Pick a
New Dream

Books by Lenora Mattingly Weber

BEANY MALONE SERIES

Meet the Malones 1943

Beany Malone 1948

Leave it to Beany! 1950

Beany and the Beckoning Road 1952

Beany has a Secret Life 1955

Make a Wish for Me 1956

Happy Birthday, Dear Beany 1957

The More the Merrier 1958

A Bright Star Falls 1959

Welcome Stranger 1960

Pick a New Dream 1961

Tarry Awhile 1962

Something Borrowed, Something Blue 1963

Come Back, Wherever You Are 1969

The Beany Malone Cookbook 1972

KATIE ROSE BELFORD SERIES

Don't Call Me Katie Rose 1964

The Winds of March 1965

A New and Different Summer 1966

I Met a Boy I Used to Know 1967

Angel in Heavy Shoes 1968

STACY BELFORD SERIES

How Long is Always? 1970

Hello, My Love, Good-bye 1971

Sometimes a Stranger 1972

NON-SERIES BOOKS

Wind on the Prairie 1929

The Gypsy Bridle 1930

Podgy and Sally, Co-eds 1930

A Wish in the Dark 1931

Mr. Gold and Her Neighborhood House 1933

Rocking Chair Ranch 1936

Happy Landing 1941

Sing for Your Supper 1941

Riding High 1946

My True Love Waits 1953

For Goodness Sake! (cookbook), with Greta Hilb, 1964

Pick a
New Dream

LENORA MATTINGLY WEBER

Image Cascade Publishing

www.ImageCascade.com

A hardcover edition of this book was originally published by Thomas Y. Crowell Company. It is here reprinted by arrangement with HarperCollins Publishers, New York.

First *Image Cascade Publishing* edition published 1999.
Copyright renewed © 1989 by David Weber.

Library of Congress Cataloging in Publication Data
Weber, Lenora Mattingly, 1895–1971.
    Pick a new dream.

(Juvenile Girls)
Reprint. Originally published: New York: Thomas Y. Crowell, 1961.

ISBN 978-1-930009-03-5

To Theresa Chiesa

1

IN her small upstairs room, Beany Malone stood in her bare feet, clutching her blue terry-cloth robe about her. Her short hair was in damp disarray from her bath and, under her ribs, small gray moths fluttered in excitement.

Dreams were about to come true today.

Today, graduation at Harkness High was behind her. Today, Beany Malone, student, would become Beany Malone, newspaperwoman. From this day, the twelfth of June, until mid-September when she registered at the university, she could give her whole day to the job. And then—why, by then she'd be so indispensable at the morning *Call* that her employer would be willing for her to adjust her working hours to classes on the campus.

Did ever a girl have such a rosy future!

She turned her attention to the welter of gift boxes, tissue paper, and snarled gay ribbon on a low chest. A calico kitten was playing with a dangling ribbon rosette. Beany extracted a flat box and from it shook out a pair of stockings. One of her graduation presents. She dropped down on the bench in front of her dressing table and caught a glimpse of her sunburned face in the mirror.

Did ever a girl have such a rosy *nose!*

You wouldn't think that one day of picnicking in the foothills would do that much damage. If only she could go from sunburn to a golden tan the way a girl should! But no, her nose had to turn scarlet. Then peel. And after the peeling, a new crop of freckles would spill over from nose to cheeks.

Yesterday's picnic was given by the incoming staff of the school paper to honor the outgoing. Beany Malone was the outgoing editor-in-chief.

She opened another box and lifted out a leather-bound notebook and ran a loving finger over the gilt letters that spelled her name. A ballpoint pen fitted into the leather loop on the notebook. Her staff had presented it to her yesterday at the picnic with a few flowery remarks and many wisecracks.

Why not take it with her to the *Call* office? She just might start work today. She found her woven pouch bag and wedged the notebook in, even though it gave the bag a lopsided shape.

The slip she took out of tissue paper was a graduation present too. She thought of one of the many admonitions to Harkness High graduates: "Be prompt in writing thank-you notes for your graduation presents. Don't wear, don't use a gift, until the giver has been thanked."

Well, Beany had to break that rule. She wanted to wait until tonight to write her thanks so she could mention casually, "I am now working in the editorial room at the *Call*."

Perhaps the friends who read it would think that she had fallen into the job because her father, Martie Malone, was a columnist on the paper. But that wasn't true, Beany told herself. It was because she had proved her own efficiency in helping a columnist get out her column.

The most popular column in the morning *Call*, which also carried Martie Malone's, was always referred to as the "Dear Eve Baxter." This half-page was made up of letters to Eve Baxter and her answers.

Mothers-in-law wrote about their sons' hateful wives; wives asked what to do about meddling mothers-in-law. Teen-agers spilled over about heartless parents; and parents begged for advice on handling ungrateful children. And there were the perennial letters from the girl who wanted help in making the man in her life marriage-minded; and from the man who needed help in winning the girl of his dreams. The letters were signed "Unwanted" or "Mad at the World" or "Hopelessly in Love."

Winter before last, when the seasoned newspaper-woman, Eve Baxter, had been confined to her home with an eye ailment, Beany had started helping her. She would drive over to Eve's house in her brother's jalopy, read the letters aloud to her employer, and take down the answers in her school shorthand. Eve Baxter even greeted her, "Hello, my eyes," and often said, "You've got a good head and heart for solving problems, child."

That was when Beany's dream of a newspaper career had burgeoned. And just this last Christmastime when Eve Baxter dropped in at the Malones', she had said, "Now, Beany, as soon as graduation is behind you, come and see me at the *Call*, and we'll see what we can work out."

Ah, Beany would be the most willing, efficient, and dedicated helper a columnist ever had! And then—well, hadn't Eve Baxter often exclaimed, "I don't know why I keep on trying to solve the woes of the world. I've been climbing these stairs to the *Call* for twenty-seven years. It's time I was turned out to pasture."

4

Pick a New Dream

When Eve Baxter reached the turned-out-to-pasture time, who would be the logical person to take over the column but Beany Malone? She would be driving her own car with a "Press" sign on it like her father's. She, in turn, would have a willing, worshipful secretary who would bring her coffee and a sandwich on busy days.

Nor did her dreams stop there. Martie Malone always said that newspaper work was the best training for a writer; and that a writer's best material came from problems of the heart. What better material could a writer ask for than the outpourings that reached Eve Baxter's desk?

So Beany kept adding postscripts to her dream. The Eve Baxter of tomorrow would say to her typist, "Here is a little story I dashed off. Do a finished copy and mail it for me, please." Or, "I wrote the fifth chapter of my novel over the week end."

When the novel was published, she would clip the rave reviews. "Here is a writer who knows the very heart and soul of the people about whom she writes. . . ." And, at the pinnacle of her success, she would be asked to speak to the student body of Harkness High. With an orchid, of course, pinned to her dark suit—and a mink stole she juggled carelessly.

The principal of Harkness was just making his flattering introduction, when the calico kitten pounced on one of Beany's stockinged feet—

She came back to the present with a yelp of panic. "Eloise! Please—not my brand-new nylons!"

She picked up the small offender and deposited her gently in the hall outside. She stepped through the disorder of her room and reached into her closet for a slim, apple-green linen. She had had this day in mind when she chose this dress for the Mother-Daughter Tea. As early as January, counselors had been telling seniors, "When you report for work, wear a dress of a solid color."

The gray moths that had been fluttering under her ribs flew up into her throat. She did have a job at the *Call,* didn't she?

On a sudden urge, she left her room, edged past the newel post at the head of the stairs, and followed the sound of a typewriter's *rat-a-tat* to her brother's room. Johnny was studying some old-time photographs on his desk as he typed.

"Johnny, you remember, don't you, that, when Eve Baxter came over Christmas, she said she'd work something out at the *Call* as soon as I graduated?"

Johnny typed on to the end of the sentence as though a thought might escape him if he stopped. He was two years older and seven inches taller than five-foot-five Beany. He ran his hands through his dark hair that, as usual, needed cutting. He picked up the picture of a pioneer woman in a boned basque and long, draped skirt, and turned dark, absorbed eyes to Beany.

"I'll bet a cookie it was brown," he mused. "They were great for brown or plum-color in the seventies. Now, what are you standing there screeching about, Beaver?"

Beany repeated her question.

Johnny said, "I heard you say she said it, if that's any help," and his attention strayed back to his early-day photographs and his half-page of typing. He paid for his tuition at the university by doing research for his history professor and helping the professor with the TV programs he presented each Friday night on Colorado's pioneer days.

Beany had no interest in dead-and-gone days. The *now* was too absorbing. She saw that the morning *Call* lay on Johnny's desk, turned open to the page with their father's column, and she thought absently, "I must catch up on his write-ups about the tornado and flood in Mexico before he comes back."

She had dropped down on the edge of a chair in Johnny's room. Oh, dear, this was the kind of slim skirt that pulled up when you sat down! She tugged at it, asked, "Johnny, how does this outfit look when I'm sitting down?"

Again Johnny turned his attention from his typewriter to his sister. "Looks like there isn't enough skirt—or too much petticoat."

"Not petticoat, slip."

"My women wear *petticoats*—lots of 'em—and they have dust ruffles on them, and sometimes the ruffles catch on the nails in the board sidewalks. And my females use mutton tallow for sunburn, and you might try that, Beany, the beet-nosed reindeer."

Leave it to a brother to tear down your ego just when it needed building up. But as she reached the doorway, Johnny turned his engaging grin on her and said with an oratorical sweep of hand, "Advance! Spare not! Nor look behind! And when you get you a job at the *Call,* don't forget to swipe some copy paper for me."

Beany went hurrying down the stairs in search of her young stepmother. She found her in the living room, trying one of her oil paintings in a wide, gray frame and backing off to see the effect.

Adair, the Malone stepmother, was a portrait painter. She was not exactly the motherly type, for she was an easy laugher, and wore a size smaller than her stepdaughters, and was far more adept with a paintbrush than with an egg beater. But, because she was loving and

8

volatile and understanding, she fitted well into the busy, open-doored Malone household.

She murmured to Beany, "They asked me to hang two of my portraits at the Wooten Gallery."

"Adair, do you have any complexion veil I could cover my red nose with for going down to the *Call?*"

Adair studied the offending member. "Oh no, honey, it'd take more than complexion veil to cover it. Have you got an appointment with Eve Baxter?"

Again Beany quoted Eve Baxter's remark at Christmastime. The gray moths again. But once Eve Baxter said, "Sure, you've got a job here," the moths would be on their way, and Beany could breathe naturally.

Adair looked at Beany's earnest eyes separated by a crimson nose. "Oh, dear!—I wish Martie were home," she breathed. "Don't worry about your nose. Everyone is running around with sunburn these hot days."

On those words of comfort, Adair picked up her portrait of a lady in a red dress in the wide, gray frame and started for the door.

All the while they were talking, a great rattle and banging was going on in the kitchen. That would be Beany's older sister, Mary Fred. No one could create more furor, and dirty more dishes and utensils, and come out with less to show for it than Mary Fred Malone. The kitchen would be a good place for her to stay out of this morning, Beany decided.

But there was Mary Fred in the kitchen doorway, yelling across the expanse of dining and living room, "Hey, Beany, is it too soon to make the fruit salad for my luncheon? You know, my Hail-and-Farewell-Dear-Companions one—although it's just hail and farewell till September, unless some of them get married in the meantime. I've been to so many of these luncheons I felt I should reciprocate."

Beany found herself walking to the kitchen. Old bubble-and-bounce Mary Fred, she thought. Asking eight or ten friends in for a company lunch, when it was all she could do to put a meal together for the five Malones.

"Well, look at our Beany! Devastating as the well-dressed career girl."

"I'm going down to see Eve Baxter at the *Call*. No, don't make the fruit salad so soon or it'll be all runny."

Mary Fred's plastic apron was over jodhpur breeches and white blouse, for she had already been riding this morning. And there were her boots, sitting in the middle of the kitchen floor, where she stumbled over them without ever thinking of putting them out of the way.

Strange, Beany mused swiftly, how one carries around certain mental pictures. In Beany's mental picture of

Mary Fred, she was always scurrying about in riding togs with her cheeks flushed and her hair wind-blown. Beany always saw Johnny bent over a book or a sheaf of notes, looking up at her with a faraway look in his brown eyes. His "snows of yesteryear" look, she called it.

She had only to think of Adair, to smell oil paints and see her stepmother in her rumpled green smock, humming happily as she painted. (But Adair never hummed when she tried her hand at cooking.) And Beany's father, Martie Malone—he, who was down in Mexico, sending back columns which Beany had been too busy to read. His was never a clear-cut image in her mind; it was more of a mood that had the smell of pipe smoke, and the warm smile in his eyes, and his voice saying, "Beany, you blessed—"

Friends often commented that Mary Fred and Beany Malone looked alike. They had the same gray-blue eyes, heavily shaded by dark lashes, the same wide, generous smile— "the Malone grin," these same friends called it.

But Mary Fred's hair was dark, while Beany's was that in-between, neither blond nor brunet, so that when Johnny called out, "Hey you, with the roan hair," Beany looked up. And sun and wind were no enemies to Mary Fred's skin which went beautifully from a rosy glow to luggage-tan by the middle of summer.

11

Beany asked, "Does my red nose sort of jump out at you?"

"Not exactly. You just feel as though you want to reach out and turn down the light."

"Honest?"

"Oh, for heaven's sake, Beaver. It's nothing to worry about. Everyone at the *Call* will look at you and say to himself, 'Ah, there goes our clean-cut, outdoor American girl.' "

"You could cut up the fruit and put it in the refrigerator, and then add the salad dressing at the last minute. Put sugar and cream and some maraschino cherry juice in it—the dressing."

"Thus spake the culinary expert."

"From this day on, I'm the cerebral type—not the culinary," Beany said firmly.

"Beaver, you know what would be fun? You hasten right back after you have your job all sewed up, and I'll beam and brag to my gang that you are a full-fledged employee of the *Call*. And they'll all think, My, what a literary family Mary Fred has. And not only will your stock soar on the campus next fall, but so will mine."

"Goof! Eve Baxter may want me to stay. She always liked me to help her on teen-age letters."

And maybe, Beany planned, Dorothy Cobb, the young society editor, would ask her to lunch with her at

12

The Keg, which was a hangout for newspaper folks. Dorothy would introduce her to the ones who drifted in . . . Down, moths, down!

A familiar *clackety-clack* at the door, and Mary Fred said, "Sounds like your ever faithful Andy. How come this early—?"

"It's his day off and he's driving me downtown." At Harkness High, Beany and Andy Kern had lunched together, danced together before he joined the Marines. Now he was stationed at the near-by Buckley Field where he could still beau her about.

Beany's heart lifted.

2

ANDY Kern in his Marine summer khakis was bending over to pat the Malones' Irish setter, when Beany opened the door. As he straightened up to greet her, she held up a warning hand. "Please! No remarks about my red nose."

He laughed and took her arm. "Can't I even call you My Wild Irish Nose?"

His starched and creased shirt clung close. His overseas cap sat at a rakish angle on his wavy, close-cropped hair. She liked the way he walked with just enough swagger but not too much; she liked the roguish quirk to his lips. She just plain liked being with Andy. The setter walked down the steps and out the gate with them, flailing Beany's legs with his wagging tail the while.

"You're nice to take me downtown, Andy."

"Nice? It's a privilege. In years to come when you're famous, I can brag and say, 'I took her down to the *Call* office the day she started there. Little did I think old knucklehead Beany would one day be—' "

What old knucklehead Beany would one day be was drowned out by the loud *putt-putt* of a power mower directly across the street.

A Negro boy of about twelve was guiding it, while another boy, with a black mop of hair, trimmed the lawn's edges with shears. The young man who was overseeing the job was Carlton Buell. The imposing red-brick Buell house was just across the hedge from the Malones', and Johnny Malone and Carlton Buell had worn a path across the lawns and an opening in the hedge from their years of running back and forth.

Beany and Andy both waved to Carlton.

When they reached the corner and the din was lessened, Andy Kern asked, "Judge Buell's son hasn't taken to lawn cutting for a living, has he?"

Beany laughed. "Oh, no. He works at a community center out in the stockyards district, and he runs sort of an employment service to help the kids. He even traded his car for a station wagon so he can haul the lawn-cutters and the Buell power mower about."

"Is Carl going to be a lawyer—and then a judge—like his dad?"

"He's going on to law school. But he wants to go into Juvenile Court work. He's a crusader for the underdog. He was telling me about it once—how his idea is that it's more important to prevent crimes than to pass sentence after the crime is committed. If that makes sense?"

"It makes a lot of sense. Work at the cause, not the effect."

Andy said as he drove along, "When I was a kid, I wanted to be a policeman and strut around in a uniform and then be a police captain like my dad." He struck a pose, leaning over to catch a radio message in a police car while he imitated the call, "Calling Captain Kern in Car 112—Calling Captain Kern."

Andy shifted his voice again: "Captain Kern in Car 112. What's up, Sergeant?"

The radio voice again: "Dead body found in an alley with a knife beside it—"

And again Captain Kern's stern voice: "Don't touch a thing. I'll have the murderer behind bars before nightfall."

Beany giggled at the act. "Did you?"

"Hah! Captain Kern never failed. . . . And then somewhere along the way I got the idea—well, like

Carl—that it'd be better to do something about the hunger or the hate that made the guy grab for the knife in the first place. Or does that make sense?"

"Yes, a lot."

"Funny, how dreams can change."

"Mine hasn't," Beany said. "I've always wanted to work on a newspaper."

"That's the printer's ink in your blood."

"And then go on to being a writer. Goodness, Andy, how we seniors have been orated at. You know, Crossroads of Life. Not What We See, but What We Choose. Holding Steadfast to Your Dream. And I'd always think that I couldn't let go of mine if I tried, because ever since—"

She told him about her helping Eve Baxter when Eve wore dark glasses and couldn't read—how Eve teased her about her do-gooding instincts.

She broke off to say impulsively, "Andy, you're so nice to talk to."

He flicked her a grin without taking his eyes off the traffic. "You're so nice to listen to." They were downtown now, and he was watching pedestrians and light signals. As he neared the *Call* corner, he said, "There won't be a place to park. You're going to have to leap out."

"I'm good at leaping."

He stopped on the red light, and she got out and said as she closed the car door, "Say one for me."

"I'll say two," he called after her.

Beany stood for a minute at the foot of the stairs that led to the editorial rooms of the *Call.* Maybe they were just stairs for the others who were hurrying or sauntering up or down; for Beany they were The Crossroads she had heard so much about.

She pushed through the flapping doors into the big and noisy rectangle. Her eyes searched for the switchboard and Ethel, the veteran operator that Martie Malone said knew more about the *Call* workers than they knew themselves.

It was the stout, motherly Ethel who had given Beany her graduation stockings, and Beany stepped over to the board and thanked her. "You're all modernized since I was here last," she added.

"Oh, yes. All streamlined and face-lifted. Electric typewriters, glass brick, and aspidistra planters. But the hot tempers and the cuss words are still the same."

Beany's eyes roved over the glassed-in cubbyholes that lined one wall. There was the black-lettered "Martie Malone" on one door. And down a few doors from it, "Eve Baxter."

Ethel muttered as she juggled phone cords, "Busy board this morning. Stop again when you go out."

Beany made her way to the Eve Baxter office, clutching her lopsided pouch bag tight. To think that soon she would be a part of all this hum and activity. She watched a girl saunter from her desk to the sports department and perch on the edge of a desk to show a clipping to the man behind it. The girl casually reached into the pocket of his plaid shirt and extracted a cigarette which the sports reporter lit for her.

Maybe someday Beany would feel that much at home here.

She stopped in the doorway of Eve Baxter's office—and drew a surprised breath. This room was in even a worse state than Beany's own room at home.

Eve Baxter was bent over, trying on a new flat-heeled oxford with a crepe sole. Dorothy Cobb, society editor, stood beside her and she smiled at the newcomer. "What do you think of those, Beany? Eve will need something like that for walking on the deck."

"Walking on the deck," Beany repeated stupidly.

Dorothy left after first shaking an admonishing finger at Eve Baxter. "Now remember!—Ask for Claire at the beauty shop and tell her to give you an autumn haze rinse."

The woman gave a belittling snort. "Thuh! When you're just an old sorrel mare you might as well look like one." But she scrabbled for a piece of paper and wrote down, "Claire," and "Autumn h—"

She said, as she took off the new shoe and fitted it into the box beside its mate, "I'm glad you came, Beany. Maybe you or Johnny can use some of this junk. Honestly, what a person can accumulate!"

Beany's puzzled eyes flitted over the hodgepodge on the desk. Pads of paper, notebooks, typewriter erasers and ribbons, pencils of all description; and, mixed in with the writing paraphernalia, bottles of hand lotion, nail polish, a cigarette lighter or two, a carved box holding stamps—

Eve Baxter was holding up a black lace mantilla. "Can you imagine that! Somebody brought it to me from Mexico—Lord knows when—and I stuck it in the bottom drawer and forgot I had it. And I found this camera. All it needs is a new lens—but I was never a camera hound. . . .That's quite a sunburn you've got, Beany."

"Yes. The *Hark Ye* picnic was yesterday—and I didn't think the sun was hot enough to—"

"That's one thing I'll miss in England—our strong Colorado sunshine. But then you can't have everything."

"You're going to England? When?"

"Leaving day after tomorrow—Sunday. That is, if I can clear my way."

"You're going to England? How long will you be gone?"

"The rest of my days, I hope. Sorry I won't get to see Martie before I leave. Tell him I'll never forget our young and green days together here." She chuckled wryly. "And tell him he won't escape having to kick in on the matched luggage the staff bought me for a going-away present."

"You're going to *live* in England?" Beany repeated again as though the words wouldn't sink in.

"That's right. Everything seemed to come to a head at once. Maybe your father told you that my aunt over there died in January and left me her home. She's the aunt I lived with when I was in my teens. Nice little cottage near Stratford-on-Avon. Prize roses. A pond with white swans."

Her restless hands kept on emptying desk drawers as she talked. She broke off to exclaim, "Ballpoints! They always go out on you when you need one the most. You could fill the Grand Canyon with fancy, good-for-nothing ballpoints."

She banged a handful in the wastebasket. "Yes, everything just seemed to fall suddenly into place. A friend of mine had passage on the *Queen Mary* and couldn't use it, and she called to tell me about it. And suddenly I said to myself, 'Eve, you old broken-down

21

workhorse, you've been on the job twenty-seven years. You've been wanting to make the break, and here's your chance.' "

Beany listened with only half her mind. The other half was a mournful dirge: *You haven't got a job. You bragged to everyone about your job at the* Call. *You haven't got a job.*

She asked, "Isn't there going to be an Eve Baxter column any more?"

"Oh, yes, and that was another break. A woman who's been running a lovelorn column in an out-of-town paper can step in here. And welcome to it. I'm tired, Beany, bone-tired. And this conjunctivitis that sounds like a part of speech, but isn't, keeps coming back if I overuse my eyes. Remember how you used to put the drops in for me? The doctor keeps telling me they need rest. Well, I'd like to putter in a garden. I'd like to win a prize at a flower show."

"Maybe this woman that's taking your place would need a typist," Beany suggested.

"She's bringing her own." She looked keenly at Beany and, for the first time, seemed to see her shock and disappointment. "Child, you didn't pin your hopes on a job with me, did you?"

And why wouldn't I? Beany thought. Didn't you lead me to believe you would work out something for me when I was graduated? How was I to know you'd suddenly decide you'd had enough of it all?

"I want to work on a paper. Maybe there's some other opening down here that—"

"There isn't. Yesterday, the city editor turned down two applicants with good credentials. Why do you want to work on a paper?"

"I want to be a writer and I thought the experience—"

"Why do you want to be a writer? Because your father's one of the most widely read columnists? Because your brother Johnny is gifted in writing historical stuff?"

Beany flushed at the blunt attack but said nothing.

Eve Baxter picked up her ringing telephone, motioned to Beany who took a step toward the door. "Don't go yet. Wait a minute."

Beany listened dully to the one-sided conversation.

The woman replaced the phone and picked up the conversation where she had left off. "Let me ask you something, Beany. When something happens to you—something like a great joy, or leaden grief, do you find yourself thinking of the right words to describe how you feel? When you lie awake at night—if you do, that is—are you turning over word pictures in your mind so as to communicate them to readers?"

"Well, no—"

"Then you're not a born writer. I'll bet your dad and Johnny do. Did you read your father's piece this morning about the tornado and flood that wiped out a little town in Mexico? No?"

She shook a paper free of the debris on her desk and thrust it at Beany. "Read it, and you'll feel the mud sticking to your shoes, and ache with grief over a mother digging through silt to find her dead children. Your flesh will crawl when he describes the scorpions oozing out of the mud and adding to the horror of it all. His column will stir up the people into rushing serum and food and clothing down there."

"I know," Beany said.

Eve Baxter pursued. "You ask *yourself* whether you're a born writer or not. Ask yourself whether you live to write, or write to live. Beany, what did you like best about working with me?"

"I liked helping people that were worried and didn't know which way to turn."

"I know you did. And you were good at it. Somehow, it's built into you Malones to reach out to anyone who's yelling for help."

"I worked hard on the school paper this year, and I learned a lot about editing and proofreading," Beany said defensively.

"You got out a good paper. I ran over some of your issues. I always read *your* columns in it." She hesitated and then said bluntly, "I remember your father and I talked it over once. How you, who felt things so keenly, couldn't make your reader feel it—"

"Did my father say that?"

"He said, Beany, that you were better at *doing* than in writing about it."

Well, thanks, Beany thought sickly. Thanks for knocking every prop out from under me.

She turned away from the desk, but Eve Baxter stopped her again. "Let me tell you something else, Beany. You like to help people as you say. There are plenty in the world that need it. But don't ever think that the ones who write in to 'Dear Eve Baxter' are the ones who need it the most. No sir! By and large, they're the ones who want to air their griefs and let the world know they've been done wrong by. But the man, woman, or child who is desperately in need isn't putting it on paper for the world to read about in the morning *Call*."

"I guess I'll be going," Beany managed to say. She wanted nothing so much as to get out.

"Here, Beany." Eve Baxter stood up and, from under her desk, pulled out a capacious shopping bag of woven string. She scooped off her desk and into it the hodgepodge of accumulation on her desk—even the black lace mantilla and the camera that needed repair.

"Maybe you or Johnny can use some of this. If you can't, there's always the ashpit. What selfish mortals we humans are. I've been so full of all my plans for getting off—I didn't think that maybe you— I'm sorry, child, if you're disappointed. It didn't dawn on me that you didn't know I was leaving. I should have realized that, with Martie in Mexico, you wouldn't hear."

The phone interrupted, and Beany was grateful. No use prolonging it. Beany Malone was jobless, and all Eve's talk-talk couldn't soften the blow.

She ought to tell her she hoped she'd be happy living in her cottage with the rose garden and the swans. But Beany could barely force a smile to say, "Bon voyage!" as the woman she had thought of as her employer thrust the crammed-full bag into her arms and picked up the telephone.

3

BEANY walked blindly through the editorial room where some of the men were putting on coats to go out to lunch. One man at a desk, evidently recognizing her, called out, "When's that tramp of a Martie Malone coming back?"

She pretended not to hear. She was in no mood for chitchat. A quick glance at the switchboard told her Ethel was not there; she had probably gone to lunch, and for that, too, Beany was thankful. For Ethel would be sure to ask, "And what are you going to do this summer, Beany?"

What indeed?

She wanted only to get away. She hurried down the steps, out onto the street and to the corner. The WALK signal was on, and she scurried across to the opposite corner with the crowd. She felt ashamed, somehow. She had gone in with such cocksureness. Had all the *Call* staff watched her exit with a faint sneer of, "So you thought you were a writer!"? She felt a gust of hate for them all—yes, even for her absent father who had talked over her abilities—or lack of them—with Eve Baxter.

That was the unkindest cut of all.

She stood on the corner, unconsciously shifting the weight of the market bag Eve Baxter had thrust upon her. Folks went hurrying by. Shoppers, office workers. The few who were alone were hurrying as though they were to meet someone. Everyone had somewhere to go, something special to do. Everyone, except Beany Malone.

She couldn't even think— Now what? She was too dazed. She could only stand there and be jostled.

A bus stopped to take on a handful of passengers. It was the one that went past Barberry Street, and Beany roused enough to join the group and get on it. She reached into her woven bag for her billfold to pay her fare. Her fingers touched the leather notebook with its fitted ballpoint and her name in gilt letters. She winced.

She became aware as she sat down of the unwieldy market bag she was carrying. On a surge of anger she muttered, "I wish I'd dumped the whole thing in the trash can. Leavings, that's all they are—her leavings."

The bus was passing the park, when Beany suddenly pulled the cord for a stop. She didn't want to go home yet. Mary Fred and her dear companions would be eating lunch. Mary Fred would say, "Here's Beany, who's launched on her newspaper career." And Johnny would probably yell down the stairs, "Hey, Eve Bax junior, did you bring me the copy paper?"

She made her way across the park, dodging the spray of whirling sprinklers. Through this park Beany and her best friend, Miggs Carmody, had driven each morning on their way to Harkness High.

Beany made for a sun-warmed bench, dropping the string bag and contents on the ground beside a flowering clove bush that hung over the bench and spiced the air. But Beany's sunburned nose didn't crinkle in enjoyment of it.

Staring moodily up the winding park road, she quickened at sight of a familiar, pale-green Chev humming along toward her. Dulcie Lungaarde, a friend and fellow student at Harkness, would be driving it.

If there was one person Beany did not want to see now, it was Dulcie with her bubbling cockiness. Dulcie worked as a carhop at the Ragged Robin on near-by College Boulevard, and always said, "Drive up to the Robin, and I'll come bobbin'." And so she did, with her pony tail the color of burnt sugar, bobbing in rhythm to her hippy swing.

Beany remembered now in a flash that she had bragged to Dulcie about her job at the *Call*. And, she might as well face it, she had been a little superior about Dulcie's carhop job.

Swiftly, Beany shrank back into the flowering clove branches. Peering out between yellow blossoms, she saw Dulcie drive by. She wore that pleased and prideful look of, "It isn't every girl can have a honey of a car like mine."

No, it wasn't every girl that could have a car of her own, with or without a "Press" sign on it.

Beany straightened up from her cramped position, smoothed out the skirt of her career-girl dress, and watched the green Chev take the turn that led around the lake.

She was suddenly overwhelmed by a "Now what?" feeling. In her mind one grim fact lodged: She had to have a summer job. It was not only a matter of pride, but of necessity. The other Malones had always worked to help themselves through the university.

Besides his historical research, Johnny picked up extra fees by writing a one-act play for the Railroad Club or the Pioneer Society. Mary Fred hurried from the campus two afternoons a week to teach a children's class in riding. For the past three summers she had worked at a dude ranch.

Beany thought back to all the talks in vocational guidance for Harkness seniors. Every counselor had stressed the importance of getting in applications long before diplomas were handed out.

Beany hadn't bothered to write applications, she remembered bitterly.

She opened the morning paper Eve Baxter had given her. She was too bruised yet to read the "Martie Malone" column or the "Dear Eve Baxter" half-page. She turned to the help-wanted section. She read all the ads through as cars skimmed by.

Experienced Window Trimmer? No. Upholstered Furniture? No. Accounts Receivable Clerk? No. A Fast-Fry Cook? . . . She thought of Andy Kern and his saying, "Limber up your fryin' arm—I'm coming over."

Interesting and Profitable Career Selling Cosmetics?

Beany had seen these young women ringing doorbells and being turned away. Besides, she wouldn't make too good an impression with her scarlet nose which later would be spotted with freckles.

She let the paper drop in her lap. Could she swallow her pride and ask Dulcie to help her get on as carhop at the Ragged Robin? But she didn't have Dulcie's happy knack of juggling trays and bandying wisecracks with the customers.

A passing station wagon ground to a stop some fifteen feet from her, and the driver got out and started walking toward her.

It was Carlton Buell. Perhaps because her thoughts were so absorbed in job possibilities, she looked at him with strangely objective eyes as though he were an individual she was seeing for the first time, instead of "good old Carl" she saw every day.

Hard muscles bulged under the white T-shirt with grass stains on it. He walked with an easy stride. His blond crewcut would, before the summer was over, be lighter than his ruddy, tanned face. She had seen him so often with her brother Johnny, who was tall and lanky, that she had always thought of Carlton as short and stocky. But he wasn't.

She asked out of her thoughts as he reached the bench, "How tall are you, Carl?"

"Five-eleven. I just took the lawn-cutters back to the center. Want a lift home?"

"No," she said in a crumpled voice. "I don't want to go home—not yet."

He dropped down beside her. His eyes went from the set misery in her face to the open help-wanted section on her lap.

"I had a root beer with Johnny, and he told me you'd gone down to see about a job at the *Call*. It didn't pan out, huh?"

"No. Eve Baxter's going to England. To live. She decided all of a sudden—So I go prancing down there, so sure that—" Her voice broke.

Carlton talked on, pretending not to notice. "So she's going back to England. I remember her telling Johnny and me about the cottage once."

"She told me—I couldn't write—because I didn't think about it when I lay awake at night—"

She bent her head and tried to straighten her crimping lips, and worked the want-ad section of the paper into a small square between her hands.

"Look, Beany, no use sitting here, rubbing salt in your wounds. Let me take you home."

"No. Mary Fred's got company—and she—they'll all ask about the job I thought I was going to get. I'll just sit here. Isn't that what the jobless always do—just sit on park benches—?"

She couldn't hold back her sobs any longer.

He sat for a moment or two beside her and let her cry. And then he reached over and shook her arm for attention. "Beany, how would you like a job at Lilac Way?"

"Where?"

33

"Down at the center where I work."

She gulped out, "I don't know—anything about—recreation work—"

"I know you don't. But we're pretty short-staffed, and Miss Cirisi *has* hired one or two high-school graduates."

"I don't think I could teach classes how to weave raffia baskets."

He laughed. "This year it's making giraffes out of laths and strips of newspaper. We need someone to handle the teen-age girls and their sewing and cooking projects. Oh, we'll find plenty for you to do. You don't have any race prejudice, do you?"

"Not that I know of."

"I didn't think you would, being a Malone."

"Do you think they'd hire me—that Miss whatever-her-name-is would?"

"Cirisi. It's an Italian name." His slow grin took a minute to travel from his eyes to his lips. "Not the way you look now. Not with that bleary-eyed, kicked-in-the-teeth look. Come on home with me. I'm starved. Mom's gone to some garden-club doings, but we can rummage up a sandwich. And then when the coast is clear at the Malones, you can go home."

Carlton picked up the mesh bag Eve Baxter had dumped on her, and they walked to the car. He transferred a stack of swim trunks from the front seat to the back. "This is my lucky morning. I not only lined up some more lawn-cutting for our Bombshells—that's our Young America team at the center—but I got a donation of swim trunks."

They drove down Barberry Street, past the big two-story Malone home where Red lay like a sentinel between porch steps and front door. Beany's fears had been well founded. Mary Fred's crowd was sitting at the outdoor table under the chestnut tree.

Carlton drove into his own driveway and stopped where the dividing hedge was high and thick. "We'll go in the side door," he said.

It seemed strange to Beany that Carlton should have to thump on his own door for admittance. Seldom was a door locked at the Malones' where there was so much coming and going at all hours. Besides, it would take a hardy intruder to get past Red who protected the Malone portals.

"Anna's one of the kind that always expects the worst," Carlton explained, thumping louder. "So she keeps herself locked in and the world locked out."

Sure enough, there was the sliding of a bolt, the door was opened a chain's length that permitted the raw-boned housekeeper to peer out. She said as she opened the door, "I was down in the basement ironing, and you never know who'll come walking in these days to rob the house or kill you in cold blood."

In the kitchen, Carlton opened the refrigerator door. "You go on back to your ironing, Anna. Beany and I are going to build us a sandwich."

"Now, Mr. Carlton, you and Miss Beany just sit down there at the dining table, and I'll fix you a bit of lunch."

Beany felt uneasy. The woman was probably wondering why Miss Beany, whose own kitchen was but a stone's throw away, was stopping here. Anna added, "I see your sister's having a party."

Carlton interrupted. "Just bring us a sandwich out in the sunroom, Anna. I want to make a phone call or two."

The sunroom was off the dining room. Carlton opened a window which let in whoops of laughter from the Malone yard across the hedge.

He said, "You know where the upstairs bath is, Beany. You'll find a squat, brown jar in the medicine cabinet. Best thing for sunburn. Wash your face and then daub that on your nose."

Beany walked through the living room with its thick-piled carpeting and drawn draperies, feeling hushed and subdued as she always did in the Buell house.

Carlton's mother was a friendly, visity woman who worked in her flower garden and handed bouquets across the hedge to the Malones. It was Judge Buell who always awed Beany with his stern, judicial air.

She had once said to Johnny, "The judge seems so much older than other fathers—than Dad, for instance."

"He is," Johnny said. "That's because Dad married young. And His Honor didn't marry until he was what he terms 'established.' He's always sounding off about the serious responsibilities of marriage. Maybe that's why poor old Carl is so girl-shy. That's why he asks you to go to these flingdings on the campus."

Beany had never had any illusions about why Carlton asked her to go to the Stardust Ball or the Spring Formal. He was too bashful, or it was too much bother to ask someone else. Neither had Carlton any illusions about Beany's asking him to one of the Harkness dances when Andy joined the Marines and was stationed for a while in California, leaving Beany in need of an escort.

There was nothing heart-thudding about a date with Carlton. It was too much like going with your brother.

Johnny had added, "Old Carl feels as safe with you as he would with his maiden aunt."

Beany had widened her eyes in mock innocence. "You mean you didn't know Carl is always begging me to elope with him?"

"That'll be the day! Why, if he even thought a girl was warming up to him, he'd go into deep freeze. I've seen it happen."

In the Buell bathroom, Beany doused cold water on her red eyes. That was really what Carlton had in mind. She surveyed the array of pristine towels and took the smallest to dry her face. She patted the ointment on nose and cheeks. It seemed to heal not only her nose but her raw spirits.

She came down to the sunroom to find a tray with a sandwich cut into neat triangles, and a glass of iced tea awaiting her.

"I got hold of Miss Cirisi," Carlton said, "and told her I thought you'd fill the bill at Lilac Way. She wants me to bring you down for an interview in the morning."

"Are you the boss at Lilac Way?" Beany asked.

"I'm the pinch-hitting boss this summer."

While Beany glanced out now and then at the bevy of girls moving about in the Malone yard, Carlton talked about Lilac Way. How, for the past two summers, he had been program director. How this spring the director had wrenched his back and had to humor it by not being on his feet more than an hour or two a day. How, even though he, Carlton, was a bit young for the job, Miss Cirisi had put him in charge at Lilac Way.

Beany swallowed a bite of potato chip. "I think they're leaving—Mary Fred's party." From her vantage point, Beany watched the scurrying about and climbing into cars. "Maybe for a drive in the mountains—No, they must be going swimming. There's Mary Fred with her suit. And, by gosh, she's lending one of them my blue one."

Mary Fred, at the moment, was tossing Beany's turquoise suit down from the upstairs balcony to a girl beneath who caught it and held it up to herself approvingly. "Mary Fred's always so generous with my things," Beany added.

She watched on until the full cars left the Malone driveway. "I can go home now, Carl."

Carlton, being Carlton, had to walk her home even though he was in a hurry to get back to the center. He reached for the string bag from the front seat. Its contents had partly spilled out.

"I don't want that fool stuff," Beany said harshly.

"Whatta you know—a camera!" Carlton marveled.

"There's something the matter with the lens."

"Look, this is a real lace mantilla."

"Eve Baxter forgot she had it. All that is just her leavings."

"If you don't want the stuff, Beany, don't think I won't scavenger it for Lilac Way. I know someone that a new mantilla would give a lift to."

At home, Beany broke the news to the family, as each one put in an appearance, that she was not on the *Call* payroll. It was not as hard as she had anticipated. They all took the attitude of, "Swell for Eve, even though it's hard luck for Beany."

She told them about Carlton's arranging for an interview with Miss Cirisi about a job at Lilac Way. She was careful to add, "I don't know whether I'll get it or not."

4

THE picnic sun, which had so crimsoned Beany's nose, was in hiding the next morning when Carlton took her for the interview with Miss Cirisi. Carlton had sent Beany back for her sweater; even under it she was shivery in apprehension on the drive to City Hall, on the walk down corridors to the recreation-center office.

Miss Cirisi's warm, friendly handshake did much to put Beany at ease. She was a warm and friendly woman with great vitality. It showed in her ruddy skin, her sparkling black eyes, and in her short, springy gray hair.

Beany listened while she and Carlton talked about the baseball schedule of the Bombshells, the swimming classes at Lilac Way, and the bare-bones budget all the centers must run on this summer. Yet Beany sensed that one flick of those alert, dark eyes had taken in every detail of the new applicant from the top of her light-brown hair to the flat-heeled shoes.

"How is Ofila getting along?" Miss Cirisi asked Carlton. "Is she adjusting any better? Or is she still the prima donna from Mexico who's too good for an ordinary job?"

Carlton shook his head. "There's something wrong with every job I scout up for her. I'm pretty sure she'll win the city high-diving meet again this year. She spends most of her time practicing in the pool at Lilac Way."

Miss Cirisi turned to Beany. "Have you had any training at all in recreation work?"

"No, not a bit," she confessed.

"That needn't be too much of a detriment. Miss Joanne who preceded you was majoring in social service. But sometimes a worker can have too much in his head and not enough in his heart. Mrs. Harper is in charge at Lilac Way and handles the play-school classes. We need someone to handle the teen-age girls—the Ho Ho's, isn't it, Carlton?" Her easy laugh seemed to fizz up from an inner well of enthusiasm.

"The Ho Ho's is short for Homemaking and Hobby Club," he explained. "We had to shorten it on the bulletin board."

They spoke of Miss Joanne again. "Seems queer," Miss Cirisi mused, "for her to work for the first three days and then leave so suddenly. Because earlier this spring when I mentioned her filling in at Carter Center, she said no, she preferred Lilac Way."

"She left without turning in her set of keys," Carlton said. "I'll phone her and tell her Beany needs them. That is, if you—"

"Yes, if you think she'll do, we'll sign her up." To Beany she mentioned the salary which was as much as Beany would have made at the *Call*. "Carlton can take you out today and show you around, and then you'll start Monday." Her smile broke into a chuckle again. "We've got every other nationality out at Lilac Way. Maybe we need someone with an Irish name and an Irish heart."

Her parting handclasp was warm as a blessing. As Beany thanked her, the woman said, "I like the set of your jaw. I don't think you'd be easy to push around."

That was a strange remark. Who did she think would be pushing around the new assistant at Lilac Way?

She sat beside Carlton as he drove under the viaduct and toward the stockyards district. Above them the sky was leaden. Beany asked out of feminine curiosity, "What was Miss Joanne like? Pretty?"

"Pretty as a picture. Blond. One of the society set that goes in for welfare work."

"Oh. Did you like—I mean, did you get along all right with her?"

"Sure. She used to phone me this winter and even came out to Lilac Way to talk over programs. The day she left she asked me to some sort of a party with her. Let's see, it would have been last night."

"Why didn't you go?"

"Too busy. We've had to line up playing fields and officials for the Young America baseball series."

But if he had wanted to go, Beany thought, he could have managed.

She pursued. "But haven't you *any* idea why she left?"

He hesitated. "Yeah. It was Ofila. She told me either Ofila left Lilac Way or she did. I didn't want to tell Miss Cirisi that. I figured maybe Joanne was just upset and didn't realize what she was saying. I mean, I didn't want it on her record, in case she asked Miss Cirisi for another place."

Ofila again!

"But couldn't you have patched it up—or told Miss Joanne you wanted her to stay?"

The iron in his voice surprised her. "I didn't want her. I told her so. I told her we needed an assistant who was adult enough to handle someone like Ofila. That crazy

44

kid is having a hard time of it. She was shunted up here from Mexico—Acapulco—and lives with her great-aunt in a little shack on the back of a lot—"

He broke off as he slowed on a corner, said, "By the way, Beany, out here we'll have to remember—no first names. It can't be Beany and Carl. You'll be *Miss* Beany. I'm Mr. Buell. Only it doesn't always come out Buell, as you'll soon notice."

He stopped the car, came around to open the door for her. "Here we are—Lilac Way."

Beany stared at the house on the corner in unbelief. It was an old-fashioned, roomy, two-story brick, covered with a coat of scaling gray paint, and with a spindly porch.

She climbed out, still staring at its bleakness. "This is Lilac Way? But I thought—"

"You thought you wouldn't be able to see the house for the lilacs, I suppose?"

"But why do you call it *Lilac* Way?"

"You'll see in a minute." He guided her up the narrow walk, and pointed to the transom of colored glass over the door in which was lettered "9 Lilac Way." "It's Thirty-fourth Street now," he said. "But this house was built over sixty years ago before the town was laid out, and the old-timers called this street Lilac Way. It might have been well named then."

45

Maybe sixty years ago it might have been a lilac way. But not now. Only one scraggly lilac bush at the side of the porch had survived. And on it, strain her eyes as she might, Beany could locate but one stunted bloom.

Carlton had to raise his voice over the near-by chug and clank of a train. "We're just a block from the brickyards, and the railroad runs a spur to it."

Beany looked across the street to the row of drab little stores; a small bakery that said "Pinelli's Italian Bread," a shoe shop, a liquor store, a barbershop. Cater-cornered from the center was a low brick building with a great activity of trucks drawing up and pulling out.

"That's the Bartell Bottling works, the home of the root beer you've often guzzled," Carlton pointed out. "Swell people. Bartell is the backer of our Bombshells. Whenever we need soft drinks for any of our festivities—or even to quench our thirst—Bartell supplies them."

Beany was looking about and crinkling her nose. "Do you smell anything funny—I mean, different?"

Carlton laughed. "No—but then I'm used to it. The old stockyards perfume. It's worse on a damp day."

The door of the gray house opened, and two small figures hurried out and down the steps. The one in advance was a girl of perhaps ten who had a bandage on her knee and limped as she ran. A chubby little boy clutched her skirt to keep up with her.

"Mr. Bull, Mr. Bull, we have waited—and we have waited for you to put a new banditch on my knee," the dark-eyed, elfin girl greeted him.

Carlton picked her up and said, "Beany—I mean, Miss Beany, this is Violetta and Vince Veraldi. Have you stayed off your knee, Violetta?"

"Oh, yes, Mr. Bull. Even when I kneel at church, I kneel on one knee. Didn't I, Vince?"

Vince nodded vigorously. "On one knee," he repeated.

Carlton carried her up the steps, through the door and hallway, and into a large, rectangular room that hummed with activity. Beany's confused eyes couldn't take it in all at once. So many children of so many different nationalities doing so many different things!

At several tables, the giraffe-making that Carlton had mentioned was going on. At other tables, smaller children were decorating plates. Not china ones, but paper or aluminum ones that came under bakery pies. These, they were daubing creatively—but garishly—with paint, or pasting on flowers cut out of seed catalogs.

Beany's eyes flicked over a piano in the corner—the most battered piano she had ever seen. And a padlock on it!

But one thing registered clearly in her mind as she followed Carlton with his burden of Violetta and with Vince clutching at his Levis: Every pair of black, brown, or blue eyes lifted in shining welcome to Carlton—their Mr. Bull.

He hesitated beside one table to ask, "What is that—a spavin on your giraffe's hind leg, Pete? Where is Mrs. Harper?"

A chorus told him that "Mizzarper" was in the office.

Beany's practical eyes saw the remodeling that had been done to the once stately old residence to meet the needs of a community center. This recreation room had originally been both dining and living room. Or parlor, they probably called it sixty years ago.

And Carlton's office off it had very evidently been the kitchen; the sink was still there against the wall, and a pantry had been made into a bath. But the remodeling must have been done on a bare-bones budget. A frayed blind on the office window. Worn and patched linoleum on the floor. Carpenter tools and scrap lumber in one corner and, in another, a black leather sofa with worn spots that needed mending.

Carlton deposited Violetta on a corner of his desk and spoke to the woman who was at the sink stirring white paste in a coffee can. "Here's our new helper, Mrs. Harper—Miss Beany Malone."

48

A Negro woman turned and gave the new helper a gentle smile of welcome but waited until Beany reached out to shake hands before she extended hers. She looked tidy and crisp in her striped cotton dress and white sweater pulled over it. Her only ornament was her wrist watch and wedding ring. She spoke in a soft, melodious voice.

Carlton's arrival precipitated greater activity. Boys seemed suddenly to push out of the woodwork with excited talk about baseball practice. The Bombshells, no doubt. The phone was ringing. A workman appeared to talk about rolling the tennis court.

Carlton handled them all with ease, as he took gauze, tape, and scissors from his desk for Violetta's bandage. He said to Mrs. Harper, "You might take Miss Beany upstairs and show her her domain while I patch up Violetta."

Mrs. Harper, too, seemed quite unruffled by the many clutchings at her elbow as they walked through the recreation room.

"Just look, Mizzarper! Felix painted the leaves on his tree purple."

"That's all right. Purple leaves are pretty."

"See, Mizzarper. See the eyes I'll put on my giraffe." And a little girl produced two red glass buttons.

"Fine, Janey. Red eyes will be different on a giraffe."

49

A confused Beany followed her through an upstairs room that Mrs. Harper called the reading room, though it had only a small bookcase of books. "We have magazines and books promised us, but no one has had time to gather them up yet."

"And these are your clubrooms where the Ho Ho's sew and cook. When you and the girls serve refreshments to a large group, you push back the folding doors and throw the rooms together. And here is the kitchen."

The kitchen had once been an upstairs bedroom. A pattern of flowered wallpaper still showed dimly through a coating of cream-colored Kemtone.

Mrs. Harper was saying in her gentle voice, "I suppose you took clay modeling in school. Last year some of the girls worked at it when they didn't have anything to sew."

"Oh," was all Beany could say.

Carlton was waiting to show her what he proudly called "our park." A breezeway connected Lilac Way proper to the gym built behind it. On the wall of the breezeway over the drinking fountain was the bulletin board. Beany's uneasy eyes read one of the notices: "Ho Ho meeting Monday 2:30."

A corner of the park was cut off by the tennis courts; another and more sizable corner by the bathhouse and swimming pool. The ground was well trodden, and a few benches sat under the two or three large trees.

Carlton stopped to talk to a boy who sat alone, watching through thick-lensed glasses a handful of children playing jacks. "Button up your sweater, Eugene, so you won't get cold."

The boy, who was about twelve, turned his beaming but vacant smile on them. Carlton went closer, said again as though he were speaking to a two-year-old, "Your sweater, Eugene. Button it. It's chilly this morning."

Eugene fumbled with the buttons, and his eyes, distorted behind those heavy glasses, focused on Beany. "This is our new helper, Eugene."

They went on through the bathhouse with its damp smell of disinfectants, and drip of showers. Under the gun-metal sky, the enclosed pool was dark turquoise in which heads bobbed and arms flailed. And by the side of it, a Japanese lifeguard stood like a watchful statue in her black suit with the Red Cross lifesaving emblem on it. Her short hair was purple-black, and shiny as an eggplant. Miss Kunitani.

She welcomed Beany with a friendly smile, asked, "Will you have any time to teach swimming? We've got heavy classes lined up."

Beany said hastily, "Oh, no, I'm not good enough to teach swimming."

The lifeguard and Carlton fell to discussing classes and age groups. Even as she talked, Miss Kunitani's eyes never left the swimmers in the pool.

Beany's attention strayed to the tower and diving board at the deep end of the pool where a girl in a red swim suit was making one fancy dive after another.

Carlton noticed her, too, as she made a spectacular jackknife. "It's all right, isn't it, Miss Kunitani, for her to practice her dives any time? I told her she could, if she didn't bother you."

The lifeguard answered briefly, "It's all right for Ofila to practice."

Ofila! So here she was in person. The prima donna who thought she was too good for ordinary jobs, who was responsible for Miss Joanne taking sudden leave of Lilac Way.

Beany looked closer as the girl came to the surface. As casually as though solid ground were under her feet, she reached up and swept her long, black hair back from her face. There was the clink of silver bracelets touching long silver earrings. Beany said aloud, "Goodness, I should think she'd be afraid of losing her jewelry in the water."

"Her ears are pierced," Miss Kunitani said. "She tells me she's worn those same earrings since she was eight. And the bracelets are locked on."

By now Ofila had ducked her head underwater and, with effortless strokes, reached the edge of the pool. She disdained using the ladder to climb out, but gripped the handrail, bobbed herself down and up and, in one fluid movement, was out of the pool and onto the diving board. Again she struck a pose, leaped to the very tip of the board which bounced her high in the air. This time it was a swan dive.

She's showing off, Beany thought. For whose benefit? For the fringe of young onlookers pressed against the high mesh fence? Or for us?

Two young boys were hanging on to a blown-up inner tube in the deep water. Ofila's wide dive brought her so close to them that a wave of water sloshed over their heads. One boy lost his grip on the tube, began clutching frantically at where he thought it was—

On a running leap, the small lifeguard dived into the pool. She reached the floundering boy, crooked her arm around him, and struck out with him toward the shallow end.

It happened so swiftly. Suddenly, Beany saw the boy standing with his feet on the bottom, gulping and snuffling, while the lifeguard, scarcely as tall as he, steadied him. Seeing that he was all right, she swam toward his playmate, motioned him to come in out of the deep water.

Carlton called, "Ofila, come here."

She pulled herself out of the pool and walked toward them with pantherlike grace.

What long black hair! And satiny black eyes. Her wet eyebrows made dark wings over eyes that had natural shadows. *Exotic* was the word for Ofila.

And then Beany looked closely at the red swim suit that outlined Ofila's curves, and she felt a wincing of pity. The satin suit had once been flame-red; now it was water-and-sun-faded and worn across the middle where Ofila had pulled herself out of the pool. Once it had been heavily encrusted with beads and spangles; but now the beads were dim and hanging by threads. Such a shabby bit of finery!

Carlton admonished her, "Be more careful of the others in the pool, Ofila. I've told you—a diver should always give a swimmer the right of way."

No apology from Ofila. Only silent, almost queenly disdain.

Carlton introduced her to Beany, added, "Last year Ofila won the high-diving meet."

"You're a beautiful diver," Beany complimented her.

"Gracias." But she didn't smile. There was even an edge of insolence in the word.

Carlton and the lifeguard drew aside to look over a list that had to do with bath towels. The dripping Ofila still stood beside Beany. Ofila asked, "You have come here to work?"

"Yes, I'm going to help Mrs. Harper."

"How many years have you?"

"How many—" and then as understanding came to her, "Oh, I'm eighteen. I have eighteen years." Beany smiled again. "How many years have you?"

Still no answering smile. "I, too, have eighteen years. In Mexico, that is old not to have marry. Is that maybe what you think?"

Her *haves* were "aves"; her *think,* "theenk."

"Why, I never thought about eighteen being old—I mean, old not to be married."

The inimical scrutiny of Ofila's black eyes was disconcerting. Beany half turned away, but Ofila detained her. "Are you friend of Meestaire Bu-ell?"

"Who? Oh, Carl—I mean, Mr. Buell. Well—yes. We live next door to each other. We've known each other since we were this high." She laughed, and indicated a foot from the ground.

Heavens, didn't the girl know how to smile? It was a relief when she turned and with light-footed arrogance walked back toward the diving board. She stopped to say something to a handful of girls outside the fence. Their eyes turned toward Beany, and her heart beat uneasily. Were those some of the Ho Ho Club she was to guide?

She and Carlton left the pool.

No sooner were they on the grounds again than Carlton's attention was sought by the workers on the tennis court. Again he was surrounded by the Bombshells and their talk of bats and mitts. He said to Beany over their heads, "I can't take you home, Miss Beany."

"I can take the bus."

"Walk down three blocks to the bus stop. We have to get the lines marked off on the court so you can start the tennis tryouts Monday morning."

So *you* can start the tennis tryouts! Beany stared after him as he hurried off. She had played a little tennis. But she had never bothered with keeping score. She had always left that to her opponent.

She stood alone on the grounds at Lilac Way, feeling dismayed and inadequate. . . . Mrs. Harper had casually mentioned clay modeling. Yes, Beany had taken it for a semester at Harkness High, and come out with an ash tray her family said looked like a dwarf bedpan. . . . Miss Kunitani had expected her help with the swimming classes. But no one, Beany knew, could work in a pool without passing a stiff lifesaving test.

She had been in the Junior Lifesaving class in the pool at Harkness last year. But it had seemed futile to work at lifesaving when she wasn't going to be a lifesaver—when her future was newspaper work.

Again resentment swept through her. Eve Baxter and her father—her own father—deciding she didn't have the stuff writers were made of.

She glanced toward Carlton who was down on one knee, measuring the court. She couldn't very well go up to him, surrounded as he was, and blurt out, "Thanks for offering me the job, but I'm not what you want, and this isn't what I want. I never thought Lilac Way would be so drab and dreary and smell of the stockyards."

No, but she could tell Mrs. Harper that she wasn't coming back on Monday.

As she turned toward the gray house, Violetta and the smaller Vince ran to meet her. "We have waited for you," said Violetta, the spokesman. "Please, Miss Beany, there is something Vince would so like to have. He would like a banditch on his knee. He is very sad because he does not have a banditch like mine."

"But, Vince, your knee isn't sore."

"Banditch on knee," he pleaded and gripped Violetta's skirt tighter.

"I told him not to cry," Violetta went on, "because you would put it on. You are nicer than Miss Joanne and we like you better."

Little flatterer, Beany thought. But something caught in her throat. At least she could put a fake bandage on Vince's knee. She laughed. "Sure, come along and I'll fix you up, Vince."

As they passed the bench where Eugene sat, he got up and shambled over to her. "I will bring you a flower tomorrow," he promised with his bright vacant smile.

"He lives near the cemetery, and he will get the flower there," Violetta said, as one woman of the world to another.

"I will bring you a pretty flower tomorrow," he repeated.

Beany heard herself saying, "Not tomorrow, Eugene. But day after tomorrow—on Monday—I will be here."

5

BEANY was not the only one in the Malone family who felt shaky and unsure of herself in her new job.

So did Mary Fred.

Mary Fred Malone had two loves: horses and psychology. She was a born equestrienne. She had acquired enough ribbons at horse shows, as Johnny said, to piece a quilt. For three summer vacations she had worked on a dude ranch.

But Mary Fred had just finished her junior year at the university where she was majoring in psychology. And her psychology professor had recommended her for a summer job at the Bethlehem Sanitarium for the mentally ill. In everyday language the sanitarium was known as Beth San, and often when someone didn't seem to be making sense, a listener would say flippantly, "I hope you get a room with a view at Beth San."

Mary Fred had reached home ahead of Beany. She called from the head of the stairs, "I just washed my hair. And I was hoping you'd come drifting in, Beaver."

Beany knew what that meant. She said as she climbed the stairs, "I wish you'd learn to put up your own hair."

"I know *how*. It's just that I can't find room on my head for all the curls. Oh, Beany, this new job! I'm supposed to know so much I don't know. I have to file case histories for patients—"

"But, Mary Fred, *you* always get by."

"Sure, sure, I'm always the life of the party, but that won't help in looking up case records for the returnees. It makes you feel sad, doesn't it, to think of return*ees* to Beth San?"

Returnees? That meant mental patients who had been dismissed as cured, but who had to return. I'm not big enough, Beany thought, to feel sad about them now; I'm so busy feeling sad about myself.

"And then I have to take a turn on the reception desk. But it's the typing that scares me the most."

"I'd like that," Beany said enviously.

"You would—you're good at it. I'm going to pry Johnny's typewriter away from him and practice all day tomorrow."

"Better practice on Dad's. Johnny's spacer jumps."

"Any spacer I use will jump."

Whenever Mary Fred was worried, she twisted her finger through a forelock of hair. She was twisting it now, until her wet hair stood up like a question mark.

"Honestly, Beany," she added, "I'm scared to death about this whole job."

"I thought you were thrilled to death about it. You said it'd be like seeing the paragraphs in your books come alive."

"That's right. But you can be thrilled to death and scared to death at the same time."

"*I'm* scared to death without being thrilled to death," Beany said. "Here, sit on the laundry hamper while I do your hair."

"Oh, now, Beaver, don't brood about Eve Baxter's leaving you out on a limb. After all, Carl's your boss now. And he's like someone in the family."

"He thinks I'm a lot smarter than I am."

Mary Fred said, as Beany fastened down a roller curl with a pin, "Dad's heading for home. He called Adair from San Antonio—that's in Texas, in case you don't know. Said he didn't know when he could get a flight, so not to try to meet the plane. Johnny and Adair have gone marketing. Gosh, Beany, with all the Malones gainfully employed, how are we going to manage the meals? Just think of all the meat loafs the family will miss if I'm not cooking."

For the past two years, with Beany going to Harkness High and Mary Fred to the university, the two girls had alternated weeks of marketing and cooking for the family. The cook of the week handled the generous housekeeping allotment from their father; the Sinking Fund, they called it, and kept it in an oatmeal box. Whatever amount was left over at the week's end belonged to the cook.

Even though it was often a chore to mix homework and home-cooked meals, Beany was happy doing it. It was a challenge to fix "cheap and filling" meals and come out with money left over. Unlike Mary Fred, Beany had a knack for it. Mary Fred always said, "Cooking comes as natural to Beany as kicking to a cow."

Beany thought now, Why couldn't I just stay home and cook for the family? I'd like it. No problems, no feeling scared—

It wouldn't do. The four or five dollars left in the oatmeal box was enough for spending money when a girl was going to high school. But not for college tuition, clothes, and books this fall.

She said on a sigh, "I'll have to play a lot of tennis tomorrow and wise myself up on scoring. You know, 'faults' and things like that."

"Faults and love-all, as I remember. I was no contender for the title myself. Thanks for the head work, pet." She twisted about and looked in the glass. "Don't I look like Martha Washington?"

"I'll be more faults than love-all," Beany muttered. She was starting for the attic stairs to look for a tennis racket, when Mary Fred called after her, "Andy phoned you."

"He did? What did he say?"

"Just that he'd call again. Not very chatty—he was calling from Buckley Field."

He did call again when Beany was descending the attic steps, carrying a racket.

She knew the minute she heard his, "Hi, doll," that he must be alone in the lounge room at Buckley. Whenever his fellow Marines were within listening distance, he was more formal. He added, "Or should I say, 'Good afternoon, Eve Baxter, junior'?"

Beany winced. "I didn't get the job, Andy. It's a long, sad story. But I'm to start out at Lilac Way—that's the community center where Carl works—and I don't know how long I'll last. I'm such an ignoramus."

"Now, now, Knucks. I'm the only one that can call you names."

"But tennis, Andy. Carl just tossed off that I'm to handle the tennis tryouts Monday morning, and all I know about tennis—"

"Want me to teach you in a few easy lessons?"

"Andy, would you? When?"

"How some girls do pounce! Let's see." He had promised one of his friends to take his place at the switchboard until ten tonight. And he was on guard duty tomorrow.

"What hours, Andy?"

"It's the old two on, and four off, beginning at six in the morning. But I can be at your service at eight after the first stretch until I go back at twelve. That will give us three hours."

Wonderful, dependable Andy. They arranged that Beany would go to seven-thirty Mass at St. Mary's and that he would pick her up there.

"I found some tennis balls up in the attic," she said.

"How long since they've been used?"

"A couple of years, I think. Johnny had a streak of playing when he got this racket for his birthday, and he used to take me over to the park with him. But I just let him do the scoring. He'd tell me the count and when I lost, we'd start a new game."

He laughed. "I'll pick up some new balls at the PX. Balls are like people—they're better with a lot of bounce."

Beany had never needed an alarm clock to waken her at seven on school mornings. Red, their Irish setter, always pushed through her door and nuzzled at her. The Malones were quite unable to figure how Red knew when it was seven. It wasn't from the sun, because on cloudy or snowy mornings he was still there. It wasn't from the hall clock striking seven, because the few times when the clock's time-telling apparatus was out of order, Red's was still unerring.

On Sunday mornings, Beany had only to mutter sleepily, "It's Sunday, Red," for him to subside on the rug by her bed.

She didn't say it that next morning, for, opening one sleepy eye, she saw the tennis racket leaning against her dressing table, and she thought of those tennis tryouts tomorrow morning at Lilac Way. As she hastily dressed, she had to whisper, "Hush, hush!" to the dog who was all whimpery excitement.

She realized the reason for it when, in the downstairs hall, she saw her father's battered grip. So he had arrived in the night and quietly climbed the stairs without wakening anyone. A pair of shoes with dried mud on

65

them sat beside it, and also a woven Mexican bag. In it, Beany knew, were presents for the family.

Martie Malone's return from a trip was always a heartwarming event in the Malone household. But this morning Beany stared at his luggage and, for the first time in all her eighteen years, felt anger and resentment toward him.

It was largely *his* fault that she hadn't a job at the *Call*. You'd think a father would go to whoever gave out jobs and say, "How about giving my daughter a try?" But no, he and Eve Baxter had decided she was no genius.

The Malones had a bulletin board in the hall above the telephone for jotting down messages to each other. This morning as Beany drank a glass of milk and ate a cold biscuit, she wrote on it:

Going to seven-thirty. Tennis afterwards. Don't know when I'll be home.

Ordinarily, she would have added, "Welcome home, Pop." She didn't this morning.

She carried her rancor with her as she walked to church. Mentally, she rehearsed what she would say to him: "It was big of you and Eve Baxter to decide between you that I couldn't write."

But it was a little hard to feel like a martyr in the crisp, early morning air. A little hard not to feel superior at being up and about while others were sleeping, or opening their doors in housecoats to reach for the Sunday paper.

After Mass, Beany was among the first to push through the wide doors and go hurrying down the stone steps. Sure enough, there was the Kern car with Andy beside it. He said as he helped her in, "I stopped at the courts and draped a coat over the post and leaned my racket against the net to hold us a court. I've known it to work."

It worked. The corner court was waiting for them.

Tennis wasn't so hard after all. Not with Andy explaining "advantage" and "deuce" and "foot faults." She wondered why she had been so stupid before. Andy played, as he did so many things, with easy skill.

After a set, Beany dropped down on a wire bench beside the court. Andy got Cokes from the machine near the gate, said as he handed her one, "Put your sweater back on. They tell me they blanket horses after a race. Besides, I like you in your green sweater. Makes your eyes green."

"I'm green all over these days with envy."

He tilted his Coke bottle, took a long swallow. "And who would Beany Malone be envious of?"

"Oh, the ones who've got jobs they want and feel sure of themselves in. Carl is so at home at Lilac Way. Everyone down there is crazy about him. They didn't take to me."

"Stop low-rating yourself. Did you give them your good old Malone grin?"

"That Dulcie Lungaarde said was like a crack in a five-cent watermelon? No, they didn't give me a chance."

"A chance? My grandmother's bustle! Since when do you need a chance?"

"I grinned at a girl named Ofila, and she glowered at me as though she'd like to throw me into the pool. And hold my head underwater. But a little girl named Violetta—"

It was so easy to tell Andy things. She told him about all the ones she had met at the center—Mrs. Harper, with her rugged but gentle face; the statuette Miss Kunitani, even the poor lump of Eugene, watching his little world from a bench under the tree.

"Beany, you misguided lug, you're a natural for down there."

Ah, but those beautiful dreams! Her own car with "Press" on it; hobnobbing with the newspaper world; reading reviews of a new book by Catherine Cecilia Malone; and appearing at the Harkness auditorium as a speaker, complete with mink stole and orchid.

Beside her, Andy sat silent and thoughtful. "Are you thinking deep thoughts?" she asked.

He grinned soberly. "For once I am. Not thinking so much as wondering—and wanting. . . . Beany, life changes, we change. . . . Let's have another workout, and then I'll have to hotfoot it back to my stint on the gate."

The sun rose higher and hotter as they played.

Again she dropped down on the bench quite out of breath. She said, "Look, Andy, why don't you go on? You'll just about make it. Let me stay here and watch and soak up a little more tennis."

"Don't you want to go home with the guy that brung you?"

"I don't want to go home—yet." Heavens, that was getting to be a regular refrain.

"O.K. I haven't time to argue with a female."

But he took time to get her another Coke, to say with gravity underlying the twinkle in his eyes, "Remember how I used to kid you about your do-gooding instinct? Maybe some of us are born with it and—well, there it is—" He added, "Stay as sweet as you are, Knucks."

6

BEANY sat on the bench sipping her Coke.

No, she didn't want to go home yet. The family would go to nine-thirty Mass. On their return, Johnny would make waffles; that was a Sunday ritual at the Malones'. And maybe her father would wonder why Beany had absented herself. Well, let him wonder.

Idly she watched two girls playing singles on the court she and Andy had just vacated. But she was thinking of Andy. What was he giving so much thought to? Or, as he said, wondering—and wanting? Driving downtown two days ago, he had talked soberly about dreams changing. And something about wanting to stop the hunger or hate that made a man reach for a knife—

"Hi, Beany! What are you doing, sitting out here by yourself?"

She looked up at the tall, redheaded boy who came toward her. "Hello, Norbett. Oh, I just needed to brush up on tennis. So Andy Kern and I played awhile. But he had to hurry back to guard duty at Buckley."

"Holy Mona, Beany, if you needed to improve your game, why didn't you call an old pro? Don't you remember that I was runner-up in the all-city meet when I went to Harkness? Then I got interested in golf and skiing. But I figured a fellow would have a better chance of getting on at the *Tribune* if he knew all the sports."

The *Tribune* was the *Call's* rival. Again disappointment clutched at Beany. If only she had been able to say, "I'm working on the *Call*." She asked, "Are you on regular at the *Tribune?*"

"No, I'm not on regular, even though I know more about sports than any man they've got. You have to play petty politics to get anyplace in the newspaper field. It isn't ability that counts," he said bitterly.

It could still surprise Beany that Norbett's dark, by-the-world-abused moods didn't affect her. Once they had. He had been her first beau when she was fifteen and a sophomore at Harkness High. And what an up-in-the-clouds, down-in-the-dumps time it had been!

She never knew when she answered his ring at the door whether she'd find a swaggering, redheaded boy on top of the world, or one lashing out at its injustices. Or one who could warm her heart by his exultant, "Beany, what would I do without you!" Or wound it by cool indifference or unreasonable jealousy.

That's why, when her ardor for Norbett had finally cooled, it had been blessed relief to have someone like Andy Kern for a beau. Easygoing, keep-it-light Andy. Not that he didn't have a hard, tough core—not that Andy could be pushed around even by his best girl. But Andy was predictable. And not given to moods.

Norbett sat down on the bench beside her. "I saw your dad's columns on the flood in Mexico. He has a colorful style, but he's apt to get a little emotional." He said it as though he were the seasoned newspaperman, and Martie Malone the rank amateur.

In the old days how that would have needled Beany. Old know-it-all Norbett. She changed the subject. "How's Dulcie Lungaarde? Have you seen her lately?"

Norbett dated the pert and pretty carhop at the Ragged Robin who often confided to Beany, "Norbett isn't happy unless he's got something to be unhappy about."

Norbett fidgeted impatiently with his tennis racket before he answered, "Oh, Dulcie's all right. Sometimes I wonder if she'll ever grow up—or use her head for something besides flipping her pony tail."

Beany stifled a giggle. "Don't worry. Dulcie uses her head."

A friend of Norbett's was calling to him to come over and play doubles with the girl players. Norbett said, "Why don't you wait, Beany? You could watch the game, and then I'll run you home."

He meant: You can see how good I am at tennis. Beany got to her feet. "Thanks, Norbett, but I have to go on."

She left the courts and turned homeward.

She opened the Malone front door, and the smell of waffles greeted her. The house was empty. But, standing in the kitchen, she heard Mary Fred's laugh in the side yard. The cluttered table told Beany that the family had breakfasted and then moved out to the table under the chestnut tree with their coffee. She wished they hadn't taken the percolator with them.

Almost warily, she peered out the glass in the porch door. The four Malones were relaxed in lawn chairs as though they had talked themselves out and could now bask in the sun and Martie Malone's presence. Mary Fred wore a Mexican sombrero of straw. That, and the turquoise scarf over Adair's shoulders, had evidently been Martie's gifts from Mexico.

73

All of Johnny was hidden by the comic paper, except his long legs. As Beany watched, she saw her father reach over and lay a hand on the percolator to see if it was still hot.

She turned back to the stove and lit the gas under the black, old-fashioned waffle iron. She felt hollow and hungry—and somehow ashamed and confused.

The back door opened, and Martie Malone came in, bearing the percolator. "Little Beaver!" he greeted her happily. "Red told us someone was in the house, and I thought the someone would be you."

Did he wonder why the someone didn't hurry out to greet him?

He pulled her to him in his old way and rumpled her hair. She hurried to take the percolator out of his hand, to say, "Here, I'll heat it for you." This was no time for him to kiss her and call her Beany, blessed—

Her father was just an older and more weathered edition of Johnny. He was tall and had the same dark eyes. Only his were bordered by a network of lines. Beany remembered that, as a child, she had thought they resembled the lines for playing ticktacktoe. His hair, like Johnny's, was thick and unruly, and was peppered with gray at the temples.

He said now, "The family made a bet that the first thing you'd say was that I needed a haircut." It was a

74

family joke that Beany was always scolding Johnny about his need of one.

Strange, how easy it is to nurse rancor against an absent person. And how hard it is to hold on to it when the person is standing beside you, warm and loving. Martie Malone reached for a cup to pour himself coffee, and she said nervously, "It isn't hot yet. Better give it a minute more."

He stood, studying her while she studied the half-hearted burble of coffee under the glass knob. He said, "I guess it was quite a jolt to you, Beany—Eve Baxter's leaving."

That was certainly leading off with his chin.

"It certainly was," she said tightly.

"If Eve had stayed on the job, she would have used you," he said consolingly. "She mentioned it to me a time or two—that she'd find a place for you after graduation."

"Yes, she told me. She told me I was a born helper-outer. But that was all. Because you and she had decided between you that I wasn't a writer and never would be…. Here, I'll pour your coffee."

Her hands were shaking as she poured it. Even now, maybe he would say, "Why, Beany, that wasn't what I said."

Instead he was quiet for a minute, staring down into the steamy depths of his cup. He even took a thoughtful sip before he said, "I didn't know you had serious dreams of being a newspaperwoman or writer, Beany."

"I was never so happy as when I was helping Eve Baxter. I slaved so hard to get out the paper at school because I— And she even told me at Christmastime that she'd work out something for me. And, fool that I was—" Oh, why did her throat always thicken and tears come at the wrong time? "—I—told everyone I had a job at the *Call*—"

"Was it the actual doing it, or the being able to say, 'I work on the *Call*' that appealed to you?"

His question cornered her. And feeling cornered, her anger mounted. "You mean did I live, breathe, and eat words, and lie awake at night coining phrases? No, I didn't. I didn't go around in a fog the way Johnny does. So I suppose that proves I'm not a dedicated writer, and so you'd be ashamed to have me working on the *Call*. And so I didn't get a chance."

She opened the smoking griddle and spooned batter onto its lower black jaw.

Her father said slowly, "Beany, my dear, you're right about having a chance. And Eve and I could both be wrong. It's just that the field is getting more and more specialized, and I couldn't see you fitting in as society

76

editor or on the woman's page or doing theater. But I should have given you a chance to prove yourself. I'm sorry."

And strange, how quickly the words, "You're right," and "I'm sorry," can pull one's fangs.

"I don't like this job down at Lilac Way where Carlton works," she muttered. "I don't think I'll be any good at it, either. I'm not the athletic type. If I could get any sort of a writing job, I'd quit."

Her father was lighting his pipe. "Right now there's no opening at the *Call*—that I know." He puffed hard to get his pipe going. "But I tell you what you do, Beany. You hang on down there with Carlton, and I'll watch for something to turn up. You know what I've always said— every experience, every contact is grist to a writer's mill. Yes, as long as your heart is set on a writing job, I think you should have a go at it. And I'll see that you do. Now am I forgiven?"

Beany smiled shakily. "Yes—all I want is a chance."

He added as he turned toward the door, "Bring your waffle outside with us. You can eat it wearing a Mexican sombrero."

"It's a little late for the hat. My summer crop of freckles is already blooming." But she laughed happily.

Everything was all right again between her and her father. He had promised her a chance to prove her talents. She could even dust off her dreams again.

She lifted the top of the waffle iron. An ivory-colored waffle edged in blackish brown stared up at her. She had forgot to flip the waffle over.

Miggs Carmody came in that afternoon to tell Beany and the Malones good-by. She was leaving with her mother and father on a night plane for British Columbia. Miggs, as usual, was in jeans and faded shirt and dusty flats. She was in a hurry to get back to their small farm out beyond the university to cut alfalfa for the rabbits before she left, and tighten the pasture gate.

No one would ever guess by looking at or listening to Miggs Carmody that she was the only daughter of a rich oil man. Today her tanned, serious face was troubled. "I wish Mom and Dad would go off and leave me home to look after things. We're leaving old Charlie to milk the two cows and take care of the horses. You remember the old ex-broncobuster, Beany? Charlie's all right, except when he's on a binge and then I'm afraid he'll forget—"

"Don't worry, Miggs," Mary Fred said. "I'll be out there every day or two to ride. If Charlie's ever too far gone to feed the stock, I'll do it."

Miggs added, "Mom hated to leave just now when the strawberries will be ripe for picking next week. Oh, yes, and she told me to tell you folks to use the chickens she left in the freezer."

"We might do that, as a special favor to the Carmodys," Johnny said.

"And there'll be more cream than old Charlie can use," Miggs worried on.

"Seeing as how he's partial to other liquids," Mary Fred said.

And when Miggs kissed Beany good-by, she said shyly, "I'd rather be going to Lilac Way than to Vancouver." It was her way of saying, "I wish my father weren't so rich."

7

THE next morning when Beany carried out her waste-basket and lifted it to empty into the ashpit, she felt the sore stiffness of all the muscles she had used on the tennis court the morning before.

Carlton Buell called to her over the dividing hedge between their yards, "I'll be back, Beany, and take you to Lilac Way."

She was ready and waiting when his station wagon stopped in front of the house later. But as she went through the gate, Carlton was climbing out and starting across the street with a dark-haired boy in tow. "We'll only be a minute," Carlton called.

She watched the two go up the walk and onto the porch of the house where a Mrs. Fletcher lived. It was the Fletcher lawn Carlton and his crew were working on last Friday when Andy Kern asked if Judge Buell's son had gone into the lawn-cutting business.

The boy's shuffling feet lagged behind Carlton's resolute ones. At the door Carlton motioned him to ring the bell. Beany saw the stout, comfortable Mrs. Fletcher open the door, step out. The boy handed her something, made sheepish explanation to which the woman listened with surprise and something of embarrassment.

Carlton and the boy retraced their steps to the station wagon, and Carlton said, "Angelo, this is Miss Beany, who'll be helping down at Lilac Way."

Angelo only raised dark eyes briefly, before he scrambled into the back seat and fairly flattened himself into the corner of it. "Angelo is one of the Veraldis," Carlton added. "Remember Violetta and Vince? And you'll have Julia in your Ho Ho Club."

He stopped his car again several blocks down on Barberry Street where two of his boys were cutting a lawn. The *putt-putt* of the mower ceased as they turned expectant faces to him. Angelo asked in a small voice, "Can I help them, Mr. Bull?"

"All right, Angelo. But one more deal like that with Mrs. Fletcher, and we get a new pitcher for the Bombshells. These people want their flower bed weeded—"

"I can do it good." Angelo tumbled out of the car. "I can tell weeds from flowers."

Carlton spoke to the boy behind the mower. "From here, Joe, move down to the house on the corner. Do a good sweeping job on the walks. I'll pick you up later. No horsing around now."

"No, Mr. Bull." It was a chorus.

As they drove on, Beany's curiosity was too much for her. "Did Angelo swipe something from Mrs. Fletcher?"

"Her rose spray. That Angelo and his sticky fingers."

"How did you know he did?"

Carlton's chuckle was rueful. "Mrs. Fletcher called me last evening to ask if any one of us had seen it. She thought we might have put it away someplace. I knew right then I had to find Angelo and shake him by the heels. I'm trying to get it through his thick head that there's more satisfaction in earning what you want than in stealing it."

"How'd Mrs. Fletcher take it?"

"Real human. She's having us cut her lawn again next week. The fellows on our Bombshell team don't have the money to buy their own baseball mitts. That's why all the furor of lawn-cutting."

"Doesn't the sponsor outfit them?"

"Bartell's Bottling? All *but* the mitts. For two reasons. A kid likes to pick out and own his own glove. It's to a baseball player what a saddle is to a cowboy. And it's just as well not to hand out everything to them. Doing for them is fine, but getting them to do for themselves is better. It keeps them from developing a gimme instinct."

He went on, "I learned that the hard way. When I started in at Lilac Way several years ago—Gosh, Beany, I couldn't do enough for them. I bought them a record player and records. When I'd see kids without shoes or mittens, I'd buy them. I took bedding from our house—"

"I think it was swell of you, Carl."

"But not swell for them. The kids and their parents played me for a sucker."

Was this by way of warning to the new assistant at Lilac Way?

Yes, because he added, "You'll come up against it, too, Beany. When you get your cooking class going and plan with them what to cook—"

"Doesn't the center provide everything? I mean, the same as the schools?"

"No, just the staples. So you have to ask them to bring extras from home. When you have a cookout, each one has to chip in—say, fifteen cents for the hamburger. Don't let them fudge on you. . . . I'm going to swing by a lumberyard to see if they've got any scrap lumber for more giraffes."

At the lumberyard he loaded into the car an assortment of thin laths and odd-shaped pieces. He stopped to talk to a farmerish-looking man, who called after Carlton as he got back in his car, "My sun-parlor fryers will soon be ready."

Beany asked as they drove on, "Does he raise chickens in a sun parlor?"

Carlton laughed. "Remember a year or so ago when we remodeled our upstairs porch into a room? And took out the big drafty windows? I gave them to this fellow for a chicken coop. So he gives me cut-rate on eggs and chickens for Lilac Way."

She was seeing a side of Carl she had never known existed before. Not that he hadn't always been courteous and kind, but so was he quiet and shy. Yet he seemed to shed his shyness the minute he drove away from the dignified Buell residence. She supposed Mary Fred, the psychology major, would say he was dominated by his pompous father.

Again Violetta and Vince were the first to greet them. Again Carlton scooped up the limping Violetta. This time it was Beany's skirt Vince clutched and repeated, "Banditch, Miss Beany," while they edged their way past the crowded tables in the recreation room.

Very carefully, Carlton bandaged the jagged cut on Violetta's knee. Beany put an imitation one on Vince's.

84

"How did you hurt your knee, Violetta?" Beany asked. "Did you fall?"

"Mom pushed me out the door, and I fell on a wine bottle that was broke. When too many kids are around, Mom opens the back door and—swoosh—we go down the steps."

Beany glanced at Carlton to see what his reaction was to such a mother. He said only, "Mom Veraldi has her throwing moods, too."

"Oh, yes, Mom throws good," Violetta bragged. "Once when Julie was in the back yard—way over where the cabbages grow—Mom threw a coffeepot and hit her."

"That's where Angelo got his throwin' arm," Carlton said. "He's the best pitcher on the Bombshells."

Violetta chattered on with gossipy bits about the neighborhood. The traveling pain of Ofila's great-aunt was now in her knee. Last week it had been in her neck. Uncle Benny was *out* again. (It was only later that Beany realized that Uncle Benny's ins and outs referred to jail.)

The two with their bandaged knees followed Beany and Carlton outside. Beany's eyes rested on the bulletin board with the chalk-written schedule of Bombshell practice, swimming classes, and

> *Tennis tryouts 10:00 Monday morning.*
> *Ho Ho meeting 2:30 Monday aft.*

"Will we start sewing or cooking today?" Beany asked in trepidation.

"You couldn't start today, Miss Beany, because Miss Joanne took the keys of all the cupboards with her," Violetta imparted.

Carlton winked at Beany. "Our reporter at large. No, you just get under way today. The Mothers' Club meets here Friday, and you plan with the Ho Ho's what refreshments you'll serve."

"And, Miss Beany, you have to go to the bottling works and ask them for soft drinks for all the kids the mothers bring," put in Violetta.

Eugene was waiting on the bench with his vapid smile and a purple iris which he extended to Beany. "For you," he said.

"Off old man Cutler's grave," Violetta commented, "that died from his stomach all knotted up."

"Knotted up," came the usual echo from Vince.

86

"It's lovely, Eugene," Beany thanked him. "I'll pin it on soon as I find a pin."

Carlton reached in his pocket and drew out a screw driver, a few nails, a piece of chalk, some silver—and a safety pin. Beany pinned the velvety flower on her white blouse as Carlton said to the donor, "Move over, Eugene, to that bench under the tree. You'll get sunburned sitting here."

Obediently, Eugene got up and made his way to it.

"Our sister Julie is going to play tennis, but she is not good," Violetta said. "She only came down because Mom is washing this morning, and she throws something awful when she is washing."

All the while the singles were played with the elimination of the loser, Beany could hear the activity in the near-by pool. That recurrent thump of the diving board, the swish as a diver hit the water. It seemed to Beany she could even hear the clink of metal, as silver bracelets touched hoop earrings.

Yes, her glance told her, there was Ofila's black mane of hair, the flash of faded red suit.

The tennis tryouts went off without Beany's lack of skill becoming noticeable. She stood at the sidelines and kept score. It was evident to her, and to everyone else, that a Negro girl, Winnie, excelled them all. She was a stunted, wiry sixteen-year-old who moved with swift grace on the court.

Beany learned from one of the contestants that Winnie had represented Lilac Way last summer in the tennis playoffs between the best players of all the community centers in the city.

"Winnie beat every girl except the one from Carter Center," Beany's informant told her.

"She'd have beat her, too," the loyal Violetta explained, "except that Carter Center girl was taller than Mr. Bull and had arms long as bed slats, like Angelo says."

The last game was nearing its end. One of the contestants was standing at the side, spinning her racket round and round. It flew out of her hands and hit a small boy onlooker. He staggered back from the blow, crumpling against the mesh fence, his hand clamped to his chin.

He was instantly the center of a concerned group. Even as the culprit was saying, "It just slipped—I didn't mean to—" Beany was thinking, What'll I do? If only Carlton were here!

She knelt down by the injured boy, whose name was Freddy, and pried his hand away from his chin. The flesh was broken and bleeding. She fought down an impulse to call to Miss Kunitani. A lifeguard would know first aid. But no, this was her job. If only she had given more attention when she had taken first aid from the Junior Red Cross at school.

She took him inside to Carlton's office and dismissed the excited audience. Freddy looked gray and faint, but he was struggling valiantly not to cry. She hoped he didn't realize that she was more frightened than he. She reassured him, "It won't hurt, Freddy. I'll wash it out first and then bandage it."

And when the bandage was in place, Mrs. Harper suggested that Beany walk home with Freddy and explain the accident to his parents.

Mrs. Harper asked him, "Which shift is your father working at the brickyards? The late one?"

Freddy nodded unhappily. "He'll be up now."

Beany walked the short distance, with Freddy silent beside her. He said only, "It's closer to cut across the lot and go in the back way."

The back yard belonged to one of a row of houses. Beany would have knocked at the kitchen door, but it stood open, and Freddy pushed in. She followed. The smell of cabbage was like a vapor in the room. A burly man sat at the table. He was bare to the waist, and ruddy brick dust colored his skin.

Freddy's mother was holding a fretful baby in her arms and putting food on the table. She glanced at the little boy but kept right on with her work.

The man's greeting was a bellowed, "Now what have you been into? Always something—"

Beany hastened to explain that Freddy's injury was no fault of his. It was an accident. "A girl was twirling a tennis racket and it slipped—"

"Whyn't he stay home where he belongs? And what's more, if there's any high-priced doctor bill, I'm not paying it. It wouldn't have happened if he'd been home where he belongs." He shifted his attention to yell to the woman at the stove, "Where's my coffee? You know I want coffee."

Beany said, "There won't be any doctor bill. The skin is barely broken. I'll bandage it again tomorrow. But he ought to lie down for a while."

She hurried out of the house and back to Lilac Way under a hot noonday sun.

Mrs. Harper was in the clubroom upstairs, eating the lunch she had brought. She said in her soothing voice, "Here, Miss Beany, I made you a glass of iced tea."

Beany opened her sack of lunch with shaky fingers. "Freddy's folks weren't a bit sympathetic with him. His father—"

"His bark is worse than his bite. Don't worry about Freddy." She added thoughtfully, "Children are made of pretty tough gristle."

Sitting at the table eating her lunch, Beany noticed something she had missed on her first hurried inspection of these upper rooms. On the sideboard in the clubroom, which also served as dining room, stood a silver trophy. It was a diving figure of a girl in the graceful arch and widespread arms of a swan dive.

Over it were tacked newspaper write-ups. OFILA GON-ZALES WINS ALL-CITY DIVING MEET. And pictures. One of the judges presenting her the trophy. One of Carlton Buell congratulating her. Ofila was certainly smiling wide and happily in that one.

Beany said, "If I hadn't seen that picture, I wouldn't have known she could smile."

"She doesn't smile at me either," Mrs. Harper said.

There were so many things Beany longed to ask this woman who had worked and observed the goings-on at Lilac Way. Yet she sensed that Mrs. Harper was not the gossipy kind.

Beany ventured, "Ofila hasn't been here so very long, has she? She talks with such an accent, I can hardly understand her."

"She came up from Mexico a little over a year ago. Mr. Buell helped her with her English at first. Then he enrolled her at Opportunity School—but she didn't stay with it." Again a thoughtful silence. "We've talked about her, Miss Cirisi and Mr. Buell and I. He thinks it will just take time for her to adjust to American ways. But sometimes I wonder."

Beany ventured again, "Is it her winning the diving championship that gives her such airs?"

Mrs. Harper's eyes crinkled. "Yes, and her dancing the Flame Dance in Acapulco and ending with a dive off a high rock. See, there's a picture of her doing that, too. She brought it with her."

Beany stood up and studied the picture that was all black with the dim outline of high rocks jutting out of the water. It had taken a good photographer to catch the diving figure, lighted by the torches she held, one in each hand. He had even caught the glitter of the spangled suit.

Beany shook her head in admiring awe. "Go*lee!* It looks like a quarter of a mile down to the water."

"According to Ofila, people fought to get in to watch her dancing, diving feat," Mrs. Harper said.

"Why did she come up here then?"

"I really have never gotten it straight. I doubt if anyone else has either. Except that her parents are dead, so that she lived with her uncle and cousins. Her uncle ran a beach hotel at Acapulco, evidently a very elegant one, featuring this high-diving that Ofila and her cousins did. But the uncle seems to have run afoul of the law—something about running an illegal lottery, so the hotel was closed, and the uncle had to take cover. One of the cousins brought Ofila up here and left her with her great-aunt."

The one with the traveling pain, according to Violetta. And her abode a shack on the back of a lot, according to Carlton. Yes, it must be quite a comedown for the diving star of Acapulco.

Small footsteps were coming up the stairs. It was the bandaged three—Violetta, Vince, and Freddy—with Violetta doing the explaining. "It is hot outside, and at home it is not happy so we came back. We would look at books only Miss Joanne took the key that unlocks it. Freddy says his head hurts."

Freddy looked pale and woebegone, and Beany had him lie down on the window seat. Maybe if she told a story, he would go to sleep. She reached back in memory to a character named Peter Rabbit who hid in a watering can from a gardener named MacGregor. She told it with Violetta setting her right about certain details.

And then Carlton returned to Lilac Way. Beany couldn't say how she knew it. Perhaps by the very quickening of life in the old brick house.

She found herself calling down the stairs, "Mr. Buell, could you come here a minute?"

She told him about the accident. "Maybe you'd better look at it. I'm not sure whether I—I washed it out with boric solution."

Carlton lifted up one corner of adhesive and studied the cut and the swelling. "Practically perfect, Miss Beany." And to Freddy, "Makes you look like a prize fighter. It'll be well before you know it."

"Sooner than my knee," said Violetta, "because you don't use the chin as much as the knee."

Beany drew a breath of relief. She had got over one hurdle. But there was still that worrying one: the meeting of the Ho Ho Club at two-thirty this afternoon.

8

BEANY sat in the clubroom with a notebook in front of her on the table for taking down the names of the Ho Ho Club, and nervously doodled with her pencil.

Julia Veraldi was the first to appear, and for that Beany was glad. She had met Julia on the tennis court that morning, and she, like Angelo and Violetta, had a warm, roguish smile. She was not one to go into details as was Violetta; she said only on a sigh, "I'm glad the Ho Ho's meet today. One of Mom's clotheslines broke."

Twelve girls in all came up the stairs and found chairs around the dining table. Beany took their names and prayed that she would soon get them straight.

There were the two Beany readily classed in her mind as the gigglers. Even the giving of their names—Sherry

Jones and Pam Mayberry—had to be pushed out through bubbles of laughter.

Beanly glanced next at a pretty, flowerlike girl with corn-colored hair and blue eyes. She stood up and made a demure curtsy and said that her name was Elena. Beany had to ask her twice to spell her last name. Zakowski.

"Italian?" Beany asked.

Oh, no, Polish, the club told her.

Five girls with Spanish names. Oh, dear, would Beany ever get Martita, Dolores, and Rosa straight? And which were the two Marias?

Winnie, the spry cricket on the tennis court that morning, came with two other Negro girls. One, Beverly, had a *café au lait* skin. The other was very black and thirty pounds heavier than any other member of the Ho Ho's.

Her name was Marcie. She added in a rich, slow drawl, "You won't need to ask me how to spell my last name."

"Why, what is it?"

"Same as yours—Malone. But I don't guess we're any relation."

Any ice that needed to be broken was broken by Beany's hearty laugh. "Your name is almost the same as my father's. His is Martie Malone. Just one letter different. He has a column in the *Call* almost every morning. Maybe you've seen it?"

"No'm, Miss, I don't read much."

But one of the girls with a Spanish name said her mother read what he wrote about the floods in Mexico. And Elena, with the unpronounceable last name and glowing smile, said she had made a report on one of his columns in her current-events class last year.

There was much nudging and snickering between the gigglers, and finally one of them managed to get out her question to Beany: "Are you rich?"

"My goodness, no. There're three of us children at home, and we have to take turns doing the cooking and housework. And we have to have jobs—and my sister never has any clothes because she has to support a Palomino mare and her colt that she keeps on the Carmodys' farm."

That brought about talk of jobs. Most of them did babysitting. Marcie Malone had worked last summer during the rush on the bottle-capping machine at Bartell's. One of them had once washed dishes at a wedding, and slept on a piece of wedding cake. Elena Zakowski worked three mornings a week, cooking and cleaning for a Mrs. Morrison who had two little girls.

"How old are you, Elena?"

"I'm fifteen, Miss Beany."

That led to everyone's telling her age. They were mostly fifteen and sixteen, although one of the gigglers was fourteen, and the overweight Marcie Malone was seventeen, and still in junior high.

It was all informal and friendly. Beany needn't have worried about her handling of the Ho Ho Club.

"Now about what we'll serve the Mothers' Club on Friday." She added, "I'm pretty green about it."

That was all right, they assured her. Miss Joanne thought she knew more than she did. Marcie Malone, the outspoken, grumbled, "She was awful biggity."

"She was awful rich," another muttered.

Again curiosity nagged at Beany about the girl who had worked here last summer, who had come back for three days—

"We make the cookies on Thursday," Elena Zakowski said.

The talk went on. Again mention was made of Beany's going to the bottling works across the street. The reading room, she gathered, was to serve as the nursery for the small children and babies the mothers brought with them.

Beany looked up to see Violetta and her shadow Vince sidling into the clubroom. The girls didn't seem to mind, although Julia Veraldi said in a big-sisterly fashion, "You needn't think you're going to hang around when we're cooking."

Plans proceeded happily about how many cookies to make, how much coffee to how much water in the big coffee maker. The soft-spoken Elena Zakowski seemed to be the authority on such matters.

Suddenly every eye turned toward the doorway and a rustle of skirts. For a few seconds Beany stared at the newcomer without recognizing Ofila Gonzales. She had never thought of Ofila—who had eighteen years—as belonging to the Ho Ho Club.

She was dressed as none of the others were. A fiesta blouse with much lace and colored embroidery, and a full, tiered black skirt that repeated the embroidered poppies. But again Beany felt something like pity to see the frayed and worn lace on the blouse. It was a dingy white, and Beany thought: I'd like to tell her how to wash it so the colors wouldn't run.

Ofila's black hair was still damp from swimming, and was swept back by filigree silver combs, on which rested a black lace mantilla. Several of the girls got up and hurried to push forward a chair for her as though for royalty. And Ofila accepted it as such. She sat down, settling her skirts. The clink of silver sounded as she pushed the mantilla back from her face.

"That a new mantilla?" Julia Veraldi asked.

"Yes. Is gift from Meestaire Buell." Did her eyes flick in Beany's direction as she said it?

Is gift from Meestaire Buell? Of course. Carlton had had Ofila in mind when he said he knew someone a new mantilla would give a lift to.

Beany said, "Ofila, we're just talking about the cookies we'll serve for the Mothers' Club meeting Friday."

"Cookies!" Ofila said. "All the time cookies. These mothers laugh and say to me, 'Is it you can make nothing down there but the little cookies?' " The very way she pronounced it, "leetle kokies," was a slur.

Twelve girls sat silent. Why didn't one of them say, "What's the matter with little cookies?"

Beany, feeling her self-confidence oozing away, said, "I've got a recipe for filled cookies, and Andy—he's one of the boys I know—says he likes them because they're so fillin'."

Her remark brought only a halfhearted snicker from the gigglers. The whole atmosphere was changed. Why were they all so awed, so anxious to please Ofila? Of course, she was older, and her diving trophy and pictures graced the room. And, of course, she had regaled them with stories of her glamorous days in Acapulco.

One of the girls said eagerly, "Over at Carter Center, they're going to serve pineapple upside-down cake for

100

the Mothers' Club. I know, because my cousin is over there."

One of the Marias added, "With whipped cream. They bake it in big pans and cut it in little squares and put on whipped cream with a cherry on top. That was what a girl I know told me."

This was the second time today Beany had heard of the near-by Carter Center. It was a Carter girl who had bested Winnie at tennis last year.

Well, Beany asked, could each one bring money to pay for the pineapple and whipped cream if they'd rather serve upside-down cake Friday?

Oh, no. It was only for cookouts and their own parties that they brought extra food or money.

Beany shot a baleful glance at Ofila who had brought about this impasse. "Well, have any of you any bright ideas of how we can manage it?"

No one spoke except Ofila. "At Carter Center it is the teacher who has what you call the bright ideas."

Little Violetta couldn't keep silent. "But that teacher has been there a long, long time, and she is old, and she knows lots of rich people that give her money and goods to sew on, and her relatives are rich and they give her flowers and even vases to put them in."

Ofila had the answer to that, too. "Maybe that is the kind of teacher we would like Meestaire Buell to hire for here." Again she adjusted her mantilla.

The gigglers tittered nervously.

Anger surged through Beany. She wanted nothing so much as to snatch that mantilla off Ofila's head and tell her she, Beany, had thrown it away. . . . She remembered Carlton's level voice, "I told Miss Joanne we needed an assistant who was adult enough to handle someone like Ofila."

She pulled herself together. "Well—" And she was certainly *well*-ing a lot since Ofila's arrival, "—we'll have till Thursday to see what we can think up. As soon as Miss Joanne brings the keys, I'll go through the cupboards and look over the supplies."

She stood up, shuffling together the notebook pages with their names. She said almost too brightly, "I'll see you tomorrow at the same time for sewing."

It angered her even more to see that the twelve girls waited until Ofila stood up. Ofila walked out without saying good-by—or *adios*—and so did the other girls. Except for Julia Veraldi, who gave her a fleeting smile, and Violetta, who gave her a full-sized one and the promise, "Vince and I will wait for you tomorrow. Now I must go home with Julie."

Beany still stood, feeling that her job was two sizes too big for her, when Carlton came up the stairs. "How did you hit it off with the girls?" he asked.

She longed to fling out, "My sympathies are all with Miss Joanne. Your Ofila that you think is having an unhappy time of adjustment is a vicious little piece."

She might have said it to good old Carl, the boy next door, but this was Mr. Bull, director at Lilac Way. She said only, "It's a little hard to plan refreshments for a club meeting when the supply cupboards are locked."

"I know. Miss Cirisi and I have been phoning Joanne about the keys and telling her to return them pronto."

Nor could she ask Mr. Bull, "How do I start the Ho Ho's on their sewing? Am I supposed to work miracles there, too, and provide the equivalent of upside-down cake?"

But she could ask Mrs. Harper later. "Did you or Miss Joanne have any plans for the girls in sewing?"

Mrs. Harper settled a dispute over a game of jacks and said, "We did hope to start making curtains for the clubroom. Mr. Buell said his aunt promised to donate material for them. But he tells me she has left for Mexico."

If only she had taken Ofila back with her!

"Some of the girls will bring material to sew on. But most of them—There just isn't money enough at home to give them for extras," Mrs. Harper said.

When the children left at five-thirty, Beany helped set the big room to order. She walked the three blocks to the bus stop.

The family was waiting for her arrival before they sat down to dinner. "How did your first day go?" her father asked.

"Day? It's been a month since I left home this morning."

She told them about little Fred and his father's angry outburst. Mary Fred told of her day at Beth San. "Maybe someday it'll be like the pages of my psychology books coming alive—but not yet." She brightened. "There's the nicest bunch of orderlies—most of them college or pre-med students, and all big husky fellows and so gentle with the patients—"

"Oh-oh! More phone calls to interrupt just when I'm going good on a manuscript," Johnny predicted.

Beany's mind was still at Lilac Way and the Ho Ho meeting. It brought a laugh when she told about Marcie Malone. She told then of Ofila in her faded, spangled swim suit, and her ridicule of the "leetle kokies" for the Mothers' Club. And about the teacher at Carter Center who was outshining her by serving pineapple upside-down cake. "But Violetta says the teacher has rich friends and relatives who help her out."

"I'll bet she's a cousin of Mr. Dole, the pineapple king," Johnny said. "I'll bet he sent her a case of pineapple."

Mary Fred said, "And poor Beany's relatives are all seedy artists and newspaper people."

"Even some rich aunt of Carlton's fell down on donating yardage for curtains," Beany grieved. "I *would* like to have curtains for the clubroom for the first Mothers' meeting."

Adair got up hastily from the table. She rummaged through the long window seat in the living room, and came back with a great bulk of folded green cambric. "Maybe this would do. There're yards and yards of it. I've used it for background when I've hung pictures in exhibitions."

Yards and yards of soft olive-green. Beany's eyes shone with plans. "Yes, there's plenty. Wouldn't it look pretty with ruffles of—oh, maybe soft yellow?"

"Hold everything," Mary Fred said.

They heard her pelting up the stairs; after a few minutes she was back again. She, too, brought in folded widths of material.

"You name it, I've got it. Here's something with little yellow, blue, and purple flowers in it."

"Oh, wonderful, Mary Fred! And the leaves are the same shade as the green for the curtains. That's the print you bought to make a square-dance dress out of," Beany remembered.

"And I would have, if I'd gone back to my dude-ranch job this summer. So there you are, pet. What with Adair's green and this, you can keep your Ho Ho's busy for days."

"But I'm still graveled about that cousin of Mr. Dole's over at Carter Center and her pineapple upside-down cake," Johnny said.

9

BEANY'S predecessor, Miss Joanne, brought the keys back to Lilac Way the next morning.

Beany was in Carlton's office, listing the winners in the tennis tryouts that were just finished. It had been the older boys this morning, the group who had outgrown the Bombshells and were called the Hikers, because Carlton often took them for an overnight trip of mountain climbing.

She felt dusty and disheveled. Eugene had presented her with a daisy this morning, and, about it, Violetta had said, "That's off Luigi's grave that got shot by a cop."

The flower by now was quite bedraggled, and Beany was wondering if Eugene would notice if she took it off, when Mrs. Harper appeared in the office door and said, "Here's Miss Joanne with the keys."

Beany looked up at the girl who clicked across the worn linoleum in high-heeled pink pumps. Her dress was a pale pink that emphasized her deep tan and ash-blond hair, and Beany's first thought was: She's certainly doing the skin-darker-than-hair for all it's worth.

Miss Joanne flipped the ring of keys down on the desk and said with an edged laugh, "I thought I'd better bring them back before they sent the sheriff after me. But I haven't had a minute. I'm helping with plans for a fashion show at the country club."

Hm-mm. How airy could you get!

"Thanks for bringing them, Joanne. I'm Beany Malone."

Beany could see her caller taking inventory of the mussed blouse and shorts Beany had made in school. Miss Joanne asked then, "How are *you* getting along down here?"

Her very tone made Beany answer, "Just fine. Allowing for my being green as a gourd."

Oh, the questions Beany wanted to ask the girl who stood in front of the desk, flapping her white gloves against her wrist! Joanne halted the flapping to say with a spiteful tightening of lips, "I see our south-of-the-border belle is still monopolizing the diving board and pool."

"Ofila? Yes, she's practicing for the Fourth of July diving contest." Heaven forbid that Beany should defend Ofila, but she couldn't help adding, "Carlton thinks she'll walk away with the trophy again."

Miss Joanne's lips tightened the more. She'd like to explode, Beany thought, and she would if I gave her a little encouragement.

Beany said, "I'm sorry I can't offer you a soft drink. The tennis players had to divide the last grapettes we had. I understand that Bartell Bottling keeps Lilac Way in soft drinks, and that it's part of my job to let them know when we're out."

"Yes, that's another of your delightful little chores. Take a tip from me, and see Mr. Bartell himself. Not Trighorn."

"Who's Trighorn?"

"He's the foreman or superintendent—or whatever— over there. And a swell-headed oaf that you'll have to put in his place."

"Oh."

Why, this was like shadowboxing. Miss Joanne tossing off spleenish remarks, and Beany feinting them. One of the pink pumps was tapping the floor now, while the next remark was being turned over in Miss Joanne's mind. It came out, "I understand you're a good friend of Carlton Buell's. I'll give you another helpful hint: That will just make it that much harder for you down here. And, of course, Carlton—the much-worshiped Mr. Bull—is as naïve about what goes on as the Bobbsey twins."

Beany's hackles rose at that. She didn't bother choosing her words, but said bluntly, "The much-worshiped Mr. Bull didn't tell Miss Cirisi about your tantrum over Ofila. Because he didn't want to prejudice her against you in case you wanted another job at one of the other centers." (Only maybe Miss Joanne wouldn't call it a *job*.)

For a moment Miss Joanne was taken aback. She answered then with cold arrogance, "He needn't have bothered. I'm going to change my major at the U. My family always said that welfare work was for misguided do-gooders, and I've come to agree with them."

"Oh." And then Beany's curiosity prompted her, "Aren't you going to work at all this summer?"

"I'll have my hands full most of the summer with the fashion show. I'm to model in it, too, because good models are hard to find."

That put Beany in her place and finished the conversation. She stood up, said, "Thanks for bringing the keys. I've needed them."

The girl said from the doorway, "I wish you luck." But there was a sneer in her words.

Beany looked out the door of Carlton's office and saw the pink dress settle behind the wheel of a pink convertible, saw the car leave with a snort that seemed to echo, "I wish you luck."

Thoughtfully, Beany jangled the ring of keys. Miss Joanne certainly took herself seriously. Could she have taken Carlton's courteous treatment a little too seriously, and been jolted by his refusal to go on a date with her? It was hard for Beany to picture Carlton in a romantic light, but she had known girls who did.

Ofila? Had her constant needling proved too much for Miss Joanne? That, Beany could understand.

Again Mrs. Harper came to the doorway. "Miss Beany, maybe you'd better go over to Bartell's and arrange for the soft drinks for the meeting Friday. The grownups will drink coffee, but some of the mothers will bring small children, so ask them to put in some orange and grape drinks."

Beany buttoned her skirt over her shorts and set forth.

At Bartell's Bottling, she pushed through a wide door and into a clanking din. After the glare of the sun, she blinked in the dimmer light and looked about her.

She saw no one who looked like Mr. Bartell, the great benefactor, or even anyone that might be the swell-headed oaf of a Trighorn. All the activity seemed to be centered about the broken-down conveyer belt that

111

carried cases of full bottles to the loading dock. Workers and truck drivers were gathered about, watching the man who had crawled underneath it to fix it.

Beany drew closer to watch. At length, some six feet of young man edged out from under the machinery. He pressed a button, and the conveyer belt moved along with its rattling cargo. The onlookers dispersed with an admiring, "Leave it to old Trighorn to get 'er goin'."

So this ruddy-faced giant who came toward her, wiping his greasy hands on fiber waste, but forgetting to wipe his face, was Trighorn. He didn't look like a swell-headed oaf to her.

She said, "It sure holds up production when the conveyer stops, doesn't it?"

"Sure does. The company that put that conveyer system in for us is supposed to keep it working, but by the time we send across town for a serviceman, our whole day's slowed up. You from Lilac Way?" His voice turned truculent.

"Yes, and I came to see about—"

"Did the campus queen get fired?"

"Miss Joanne? No, she quit. So I came to see about the drinks for the Mothers' Club—"

"You ordering them or asking for them?"

Beany looked at his belligerent, black-smudged face and laughed. "I'm asking for them, kind sir. Here, give me that waste, and I'll rub the grease off your forehead and one ear."

A half smile threatened. "I didn't mean to act so crabby, Miss—Miss—"

"I'm Beany Malone."

He still regarded her mistrustfully. "Maybe you're one of these college girls that thinks everybody that never set foot in their ivy halls is dirt under their feet. Well, I started working here ten years ago when I was twelve. After school and on week ends. And when I was a soph in high school, I worked here all that summer on the capping machine. So I just decided not to go back and waste time when none of it was soaking in anyway. So you see I'm just a big, dumb cluck to the college girls that sashay around at Lilac Way."

Beany felt new anger at Miss Joanne for her attitude toward this hard-working, young fellow. "Dumb? You must be pretty smart to run this whole bottling works for Bartell."

"There's a lot to keeping all this machinery moving, so's to keep the trucks loaded and fanning out all over town. Why, Miss, there ain't nothing with moving parts I can't fix."

"Is that so!" she said, and thought: Ah, let him brag—he'll feel better.

"Look here." He guided her to the door and pointed to a long and rather rakish car at the curb. "See that Merc? That was the boss's. He had it three years and had nothing but grief with it. A rattle here, a birdie there. It stalled when it was cold, and got so hot it all but melted down when he drove it in the mountains. He was ready to push it off a cliff. So he sold it to me cheap. So I tinker on it a few days, and now she purrs like a contented teakettle. All I have to do is drive a car around a block to know what the trouble is."

"I wish you could drive Johnny's around the block for him. He's my brother, and the hind wheel of his car just goes dead on him ever so often."

"Could be a lot of things," Trighorn muttered. He studied Beany's friendly, freckled face for a moment as though he wanted to suggest something. Instead he said, "I guess you'll want about two cases for your club meeting, huh?"

"Whatever you think, Mr. Trighorn."

He went through the act of looking behind him and around him. "I'm trying to find that Mister you was talking to."

Beany's eyes danced. "All right, Trighorn. And Mrs. Harper said it would be nice to have some grape and orange for the little children the mothers will bring."

"I'll put in a dozen of a new lime drink we got, too. I better make it two dozen. I figure the refrigerator upstairs and the box in Buell's office are empty by now."

"Yes, we used the last. But that's all right—I mean, you don't have to keep Lilac Way supplied, do you?"

He waved his hand largely. "That neighborhood house is Bartell's baby. Besides, he takes it off his income tax. No, I figured you were running dry over there," his eyes took on their malicious gleam again, "but I wanted to give Miss Hoity-toity a bad time and make her come over and ask for it. It'll be different with you."

They parted on a friendly, "Be seeing you."

It was not quite time for the sewing session of the Ho Ho's, and Beany was on a high stool measuring the windows, when Trighorn came up the stairs lightly carrying a case of soft drinks on his shoulder.

"I'm loading up your icebox." He grinned. "Want me to open one for you? That new lime one I was telling you about?"

"I'd love it, Trighorn."

She perched on the stool and drank it with thirsty appreciation.

He stood, shuffling his feet a moment before he said, "I was just thinking. I could drive you home after work and take a look at your brother's car. That is, if you want to." The last was said with that same challenging air.

That's it, Beany thought suddenly. I'll bet he offered to drive Miss Joanne home and she snubbed him royally. Beany said with honest delight, "Would you, Trighorn? That'd sure be nice of you. And you can have supper with us."

"I ain't trying to mooch a meal," he said defensively.

"I'm not even sure it'll be a meal." Beany laughed. "Not since my sister and I are both working. But someone usually puts on something to cook."

His bravado dropped, and he was suddenly just a young man who'd had more work than play in his life. He looked wonderingly at Beany. "You're different. Funny, how a lot of girls never want you to meet their folks. They figure a guy like me is good enough to spend dough on them—oh sure, all the traffic will bear—but they don't ask me to visit them. What time are you through here?"

"About five-thirty."

"I'll be by."

Beany phoned home and on her third try got Johnny who said, "Answering service for Malones Incorporated."

He was delighted when she told him she was bringing home a mechanic to diagnose his wheel trouble. "Fine. Right now I've got a pioneer wife who's fighting her way through a blizzard back to her soddy and her seven-week-old baby. But if I can get her back in another page or two, I'll go out to the Carmodys' for a hen to cook. Remember Miggs told us please to use up the ones they had to leave in the freezer?"

When the Ho Ho's filtered up the stairs and into the clubroom that afternoon, Beany met them with her yard goods, her curtain plans, and her enthusiasm. She shook out the soft green cambric and explained how she had come by it.

"And this flowered print my sister bought for a square-dance dress. She bought even more than a dress would take—to allow for mistakes, she said. See how pretty the yellowish ruffles will look on the soft green."

Elena Zakowski's blue eyes shone. "Wait till I tell Mama that she will be surprised when she comes to the meeting. But I won't tell her what the surprise is."

"Don't any of you tell," Beany enjoined. "Let's surprise all the mothers."

If only Ofila had stuck to her diving board and stayed away from the Ho Ho meeting. But there she was, saying, "At my uncle's hotel in Acapulco the curtains are all of silk."

Beany was sorely tempted to say, "This isn't your *onkel's 'otel* with its *seelk* curtains." But she went on, "And if I've figured right, there'll be enough of this yellow print for ruffles, and a piece left over for a tablecloth."

117

"Tablecloth!" Ofila put in. "Where I come from, we would not make tablecloth from goods that was meant for dress."

Beany demonstrated how the flowered print would look on the long table. . . . She thought wryly: It's like a tug of war, with Ofila trying to pull the girls on her side, and my yanking them back. She gave Ofila a narrow glance. *Don't think I'll give an inch, sister.*

"And we'll have a big flower centerpiece in the middle of the table," she planned on. "Do any of you girls have flowers at home you can bring?"

The ubiquitous Violetta and her shadow Vince had slipped up the stairs again. She contributed, "There are flowers in the cemetery to pick. The dead ones don't care if you do."

Elena Zakowski said, "I can ask Papa for some of his peonies."

Beany's enthusiasm won the tug of war that afternoon. Elena, the competent one, helped Beany measure and cut widths. The gigglers giggled and tore strips which the others gathered into ruffles. One of the two Marias sat at a noisy machine, and Winnie bent her sharp, earnest face over the second.

And through it all was Violetta's praiseful chant, "It will look so pretty. At Carter Center they do not have green curtains with ruffles with little flowers."

But the teacher at Carter Center, with her rich connections, was serving the Mothers' Club more than little cookies. As Beany basted on ruffles, she kept thinking about that.

She had unlocked the cupboards and taken minute inventory. A goodly supply of staples, but no luxury items. She wondered if she couldn't buy the pineapple herself. But no, that was what Carlton had warned her against. "Doing for them is fine, but getting them to do for themselves is better."

By working late, they finished one pair of curtains that afternoon. "We'll wait until both pairs are done to press them," Beany said as they sat back and drank the lime drink Trighorn had brought.

This time when the girls left, they said from the top of the stairs, "G'bye, Miss Beany," and some added, "We'll come early tomorrow, so's to be sure the curtains and tablecloth are done in time for the party Friday."

"We'll have Thursday too," Beany reminded them.

Ofila got in a parting supercilious shot. "Thursday, we will have to make those little cookies."

10

IN the Malone household, one never knew how many places to set at the table until a last-minute count was made.

Martie Malone, the columnist, often turned away from the phone to say, "I have to catch the first plane to the West Coast to cover the strike." And often when he had been gone awhile, one of the young Malones would glance out as a taxi stopped, and announce, "Well, look who's climbing out! Pappy, no less." Johnny referred to him as "Our off-again, on-again, gone-again father."

When he was home, he was apt to phone from the *Call* office and say, "An old reporter friend of mine from Chicago just strayed in. How about my bringing him home?"

The Malone stepmother, too, with her commissions for portraits, her exhibits in out-of-town galleries, often had to pack her easel, paints, and overnight bag for short trips.

And when she was home, it was not unusual for one of her artist friends to linger on in the living room until Adair hurried out to say to the cook of the week, "Do you suppose I could ask Carmen—?"

The answer was always, "Oh, sure."

Johnny, the hospitable, was always bringing friends in, either to raid the refrigerator or to wait for a meal. And Mary Fred often lamented, "How come other girls have dates that wine and dine them, and I always get the hungry, impoverished type that are working their way through school?"

Add to that Miggs Carmody who stayed the night when she double-dated with Beany; and Dulcie Lungaarde who came to the Malones', after a stint at the Ragged Robin, to dress for dates, because her own home was far out on the edge of town.

No, there was nothing routine about the Malone household.

This evening Trig, with Beany beside him, had no sooner driven into the Malone driveway than Johnny came to meet them, followed by an old fellow, weaving a bit crookedly on his cowboy boots. Johnny explained in a low voice, "I brought old Charlie back along with the stewing hen before he got himself stewed."

He shook hands with Trighorn. "Beany tells me you're a whiz at doctoring up cars. I've got a hundred-mile drive out on the plains to interview an old-timer and—"

"He helps with a TV show about old-timers," Beany put in.

"And I'll be in a heck of a spot if that hind wheel goes dead on me."

"Does it happen when you've driven awhile and the car heats up?" Trighorn asked.

"Yeah, come to think of it, it does."

"Could be the emergency brake cable. Let me take a look."

Johnny said generously to the old cowhand, "Stick around, Charlie, and give us a hand."

You certainly never knew how many to set the table for at the Malones.

Beany went into the kitchen and the din of Mary Fred extracting a muffin pan from the pan closet. Dulcie Lungaarde was sitting on a kitchen stool in the carhop togs she wore at the Ragged Robin, taking swift stitches on something coral-colored and white polka-dotted in her lap.

Mary Fred yelled over her clatter, "Our aged parents have been invited out for dinner. And Dulcie's telling me how to make blueberry muffins so I can impress the male that Johnny said you were bringing home."

Dulcie snipped a thread and asked with a predatory gleam, "Who is he, how old is he, and what does he look like?"

"Trighorn, twenty-two, and take a look at him yourself."

Both Mary Fred and Dulcie peered out the window, and Mary Fred said, "All I can see is a pair of number twelves sticking out from under Johnny's car."

Dulcie explained that Tuesday was her night to get off early at the Ragged Robin, and she had to put the hem in the dress she was going to wear on a date at seven or thereabouts.

"Norbett?" Beany asked.

"Yeah, same old throw-his-weight-around Norbett."

"Try and give him a better outlook on life," Beany said. "He was working at being one of the angry young men when I saw him at the park Sunday."

"He wouldn't have to work very hard," Dulcie muttered.

"Going dancing?" Mary Fred asked.

"I should hope so. It isn't a date in my book, if I don't. No, Mary Fred, don't put the blueberries in till the last. Honestly!—These full skirts are a mile around when you're in a hurry. Beany, do something with your little cat so it won't play hide-and-seek in this dress I'm trying to hem."

Beany fed the small calico kitten on the back porch and closed the door on it.

Mary Fred warned, "Now, Beaver, don't spend time fancying up the chicken. Because we want to have dinner without delay and take Charlie back to the Carmody place in time for chores. He isn't quite as wobbly on his feet as he was before Johnny poured hot coffee down him."

The muffins were out of the oven, Dulcie was pressing her dress in the butler's pantry, and Beany was setting the table for the assorted six, when the three males came in. Johnny was jubilant. It *was* the emergency brake cable that had been contracting in heat and tightening its hold on the hind wheel, and Trighorn had loosened it.

He took their praises with an "Aw, it was nothin' " shyness. "You'd better try it out first before you start your long drive, Johnny," he advised.

"We'll all try it out tonight, driving out to the Carmodys'," Mary Fred said.

Old Charlie sat grumpily at the head of the table, looking as though he wished he were back in the tavern

Johnny had routed him out of. And Dulcie. It surprised Beany that she didn't turn on her charm for Trighorn. But she sat studying him and not once interrupting the car talk between him and Johnny.

Trighorn, his flashy plaid jacket back in place, was ill at ease at the table. He speared a blueberry muffin with his fork, looked around as though he feared his technique was wrong. Johnny picked up his fork and speared one, too.

Dulcie was the first to leave the table. "Got to get prettied up," she muttered.

They were still sipping iced tea when she made a breath-taking reappearance. The dress she had been whipping the hem in was a low-necked bouffant. The lipstick she had applied generously was the same bright coral. The mascara treatment, as well as the fan-shaped crystal earrings, brought out the sparkle of her eyes. Her burnt-sugar pony tail bobbed with each prancy step of high heels.

Almost in one voice Mary Fred and Beany breathed out, "Pretty, pretty!" and Johnny with a poetic gesture quoted, " 'She walks in beauty like the night.' "

"I walk in bargain basement remnants," Dulcie said. "I found two pieces of this polka-dot stuff that matched, and one was a dollar nineteen, and the other a dollar twenty-seven. Put them all together, and here I am. And then I passed a counter where purses were stacked high and I found this one to match."

"Is that a purse?" Johnny asked of the large plastic one she held up. "I thought it was a duffel bag."

Dulcie sat gingerly on the edge of a chair, so as not to muss her skirt, and started to transfer the contents of her old purse to the new. She worked unsuccessfully at the fastening. She muttered, "It worked all right at the store."

Johnny reached for it, tried also to open it without success. Mary Fred said, "I'd take it back," and Dulcie confessed, "It was the kind of sale that said no returns."

Trighorn stretched out his big-knuckled hand for it. He studied the recalcitrant catch, held it to his ear and rocked it back and forth. "I know what's the matter with it. I could fix it in a minute with the tools I got at home."

Beany said, "And you could give it to me, and I could bring it back to her."

"You're quite the fixer, aren't you?" Dulcie said to Trighorn with her most dazzling smile.

He gave her a sober look. "When you don't have the dough to buy new, you learn to fix the old."

Her bright pertness slid away from her. "That's right. And when you don't have money to buy what you want, you hunt for marked-down ones."

The doorbell soon rang, and Dulcie said, "That's my date. Good-by all."

Beany followed behind her to turn on the porch light. She heard Norbett's greeting, "Holy Mona, Dulcie! Where do you think you're going? The firemen's ball?"

And then Mary Fred was hurrying them out to Johnny's car that looked pretty scuffy beside Trighorn's. Old Charlie went with alacrity, anxious to be free of the young folks to follow his own pursuits.

They were climbing into the car when Carlton Buell came through the hedge. He had taken pictures of the Bombshells he wanted Johnny to help him develop.

"Come on with us out to the Carmodys'," Johnny urged. "You need to get away from your center and see how the other half lives."

So Carlton climbed into the front seat with Johnny and Trighorn to check with them on the emergency brake cable.

Beany and Mary Fred sat in back with Charlie, who aired his grievances all the way to the Carmody place. Horses, he didn't mind taking care of. But a cow. That was insult to his broncobusting soul. Not so much the feeding, or even milking—"But there's all that milk and cream to fiddle with and have it stacking up in the icebox."

127

The sun was making its final crimson splash in the sky when Johnny directed Trighorn to turn off the highway and take the lane that led past the Carmody strawberry patch in front of the rambling, green frame house. Charlie was still grumbling as he climbed out. He motioned toward the patch and snorted, "Strawberries. I told Mrs. Carmody I'd leave 'em for the birds. I'm no berry picker."

Beany stood beside the car and stared down at the patch where small spots of red showed among the green foliage. "Strawberry shortcake," she yelled shrilly. "Johnny, Mary Fred, all of you—strawberry shortcake for the Mothers' Club. Somehow, we'll get out and pick—"

Mary Fred and Johnny stood for only one dazed second, and then let out a whoop of joy. "Sure. Strawberry shortcake."

They turned foolish and zany. They chanted a Te Deum: "Strawberry shortcake. With whipped cream on top. Whoopee! We will save Beany's honor—and all of the Malones'—"

Johnny came in with his bass, "We will show Mrs. Cousin-of-Dole-pineapple. Whoopee!"

Trighorn caught the spirit of it, and so did Carlton. He shouted in tune, "You can bring the Ho Ho's out—to pick your strawberries—"

128

Old Charlie didn't quite know what it was all about, but he came in on the last "'Whoopee," and added, "If it's whipped cream you want, you can take the whole pesky batch."

11

THE berry-picking outing to the Carmody farm was all the Ho Ho's could talk about the next day when they stitched and ruffled the second pair of curtains. Carlton had offered his station wagon for conveyance. Even that was not adequate for the thirteen club members and Beany, driver.

And Violetta who pleaded with her heart in her eyes, "I would not take up much room, Miss Beany, and Vince can sit on my lap. I have never seen a strawberry patch. We have only cabbages and garlic in our garden."

The Malone stepmother came to the rescue by saying she could take five in her yellow convertible.

The Ho Ho's were to gather at Lilac Way for the outing the next afternoon. Elena Zakowski was the first to appear, and with her was her older brother Oleg. He was one of the Hikers whose tennis score Beany had kept earlier in the week.

He tipped his cap to Beany, said, "My father wanted me to ask you about this trip Elena wants to take this afternoon."

Beany explained it all; the berry-picking at the Carmody farm for the strawberry shortcake for the Mothers' Club meeting the next day.

This did not quite satisfy the sober young man who was on his way back to his shift at the brickyards. "My father thinks you are very young, Miss Beany. And that Elena should not go unless there is somebody older."

"Oh!" And then, "But there is somebody older, Oleg. Adair. She's my stepmother. I guess Elena didn't understand. Because we all call her Adair."

"But she is Mrs. Malone?"

"Yes, she is Mrs. Malone."

His frown of worry turned into a smile. "Then my father will consent to Elena's going. Elena, you will ride with Mrs. Malone. Then everything will be all right with Papa."

Elena nodded happily, as though she were used to the men in the family making the decisions.

Violetta, who held tight to Beany's flowered cotton skirt as though she feared she might somehow be left, confided as Oleg strode off, "Polish papas are awful strict."

And Beany had sometimes thought her father old-fashioned in the matter of chaperones!

Two cars full of gay and chattering girls wove their way through the city, out beyond the university, and toward the mountains. (Beany had seen to it that Ofila also rode with Mrs. Malone.)

At the Carmody farm the girls were out of the cars and into the strawberry patch like a flock of magpies. Beany and Adair smiled happily at each other.

For a brief moment that afternoon, Beany's heart went out in sympathy to Ofila. She stood in the strawberry patch, somehow a little less glamorous and more childish than she appeared at Lilac Way, and looked toward the mountains looming high in the west. "We have much mountains in Mexico," she said with a nostalgic catch in her voice. "In Acapulco they go right into the ocean."

"Are you still homesick for Mexico, Ofila?" Adair asked.

She answered on a sigh, "My great-aunt's house is so very little. Two room. I do not like so little house."

Beany admonished the pickers, "Fill the boxes first—and then help yourselves to any that are left."

As the berries filled the shoe boxes, she told them about Miggs Carmody and their being little girls together, and how Miggs's mother always asked all the Malones and Carlton Buell out for "Strawberry Day," when they could eat all the berries they wanted.

She added on a laugh, "Car—I mean, Mr. Buell—always called it 'Stomach-ache Day.'"

Ofila flung out, "Always you brag about you know Meestaire Buell so much better than anybody."

Beany might have made angry answer, but Adair said gently, "He lives next door to us, Ofila. He goes to school with Beany's brother Johnny. They are always together."

They had to race a thundershower with their picking. They ran for shelter to the Carmody back porch and kitchen, and Beany made chocolate with some of the milk Charlie grumbled about. He was nowhere in evidence.

With their boxes full of berries, with one of the Marias holding a bouquet of yellow iris, and the girls not quite so talkative, the two cars retraced the long route back to Lilac Way.

Beany was late coming home the next evening after her first social event at Lilac Way. The Mothers' Club had lingered long. She was late for her date with Andy Kern, who visited with the family while he waited.

Another visitor sat upright in one of the slanting-backed chairs in the side yard—a huge, raw-boned man in clerical black, who got up and squeezed Beany's hand between his two great paws, and lifted a bushy eyebrow to say, "So it's *Miss* Beany now, I hear. And how was your party?"

His Irish brogue put at least three *r's* in *party*.

This was Father Hugh, whose parish was in Twin Pines some thirteen miles out of town in the foothills. But he also ran a mission in the poorest part of Denver, so that when he stepped in the Malone front door with his "God bless this house," Martie Malone always called out, "Here's Father Hugh. Lock up the icebox and hide your shoes, everyone."

Seldom did the priest take his leave that he didn't say, "Would you happen to have a stray blanket for a poor family that shivers through the night?" Or, "I know a wisp of a girl, Beany, that could wear any shoes you've outgrown."

Before Beany could answer the priest, Johnny said, "Tell us quick. Were the mothers shattered by your shortcake?"

134

Indeed, yes, and by the new curtains, yellow print tablecloth, flower centerpiece, and the coffee urn that she had taken off the Malone sideboard, Beany assured him.

"Did Miss Malone sit behind it and pour?" Mary Fred asked.

"Heavens, no. I was tearing around, warming babies' bottles, and opening grapettes and orange crushes, and trying to figure out which mother belonged to which Ho Ho. Señorita Ofila Gonzales presided behind the coffee urn."

Ah, that was still a raw spot! But she wouldn't tell about it, or even think of it now. She hurried to tell her father how adept his almost namesake, Marcie Malone, was at quieting all the small tots in the nursery, while the club meeting was held downstairs.

Andy stood up and pulled her out of her slanting-backed chair in which she was stretched full length. "Come on, Miss Beany. I'll buy you a frosted malt at the Ragged Robin."

"But not strawberry," she said.

At the drive-in, Dulcie Lungaarde came to take their order. She was not in one of her best moods, and when Beany asked her if she could save paper plates for the young artists at Lilac Way, she snapped, "Oh, for Pete's sake, Beany! I should hang over the counterman as he cuts pies, and catch the plates before they land in the trash can!"

A few minutes later when Dulcie brought back their malts on a tray and clamped it on their car, Beany said, "You looked mighty pretty in your new dress the other night, Dulcie."

Even that didn't lift her spirits. She gave a grunting, "I looked like an overdressed carhop to some," and went on to her other customers.

Beany and Andy gurgled their creamy drinks through straws, talked in snatches or sat in weary silence. Andy had just finished another stint of guard duty on the gate. He asked her if the throwing Mom Veraldi had come to the party, and Beany chuckled and said yes.

"She's fat and has the heartiest laugh. Violetta was so proud of her because she wore the biggest hat with the most flowers on it. You can't really blame Mom for throwing when the clothesline broke, because there's going to be another little Veraldi before long."

"If there's anything in prenatal influence, he—if it is a he—will be another pitcher for the Bombshells," Andy said.

Dulcie returned to take Andy's money and unclamp the tray. She stood balancing it to ask, "Well, could the great fixer Trighorn do anything with my bargain bag or not?"

"I don't know, Dulcie. I saw him yesterday, and he says, with all this hot weather, they're having to run a night shift to keep trucks delivering their orders."

Without a word, Dulcie walked off. But her hippy swing and the flirty bounce of her pony tail were lacking.

Andy drove down Barberry Street and stopped at the curbing in front of the Malone house. He said as he walked her through the gate, "What do you suppose is eating Dulcie?"

"Probably a fight with Norbett," Beany hazarded.

When Andy was gone, she stood on alone in the front hall, quieting Red who whimpered in as much delight as though she had been gone a month. She leaned against the newel post, patting his broad head. . . .

Because something was eating Beany. Something she had stopped short of telling the family when she told them of Ofila presiding behind the coffee urn.

Beany had planned to give Elena Zakowski that honor. Elena—always smiling, always willing—had done more than her share of hulling berries, shining silver, washing windows. This morning she had got up at dawn and taken the long bus ride to the Morrisons' where she worked so that she could cook and clean for them and still be back at Lilac Way in time to help with the shortcake and measure coffee and water in the coffee maker.

137

She had brought Papa's white peonies to mix with the yellow iris, and taken great pains with the centerpiece.

The one who had hampered more than helped was Ofila Gonzales. She had made a late appearance in the clubrooms in her Acapulco finery. This time it was a yellow silk dress trimmed in black lace, and sadly in need of pressing. And the black lace mantilla.

Beany had filled the urn in the kitchen, carried it in to the table, and, looking about for Elena, told her to smooth back her hair and sit down behind it. But Elena shrank back. "Oh no, Miss Beany—no, I shouldn't be the one to sit down and pour."

"Why not?" Beany wanted to know.

A constrained silence fell on all the girls who were bustling about. They looked at Ofila, at Beany—looked away. The gigglers snickered uneasily, and Julia Veraldi volunteered, "When Ofila went to the bullfights in Mexico City, she always sat in the president's box. She showed us pictures."

So that was it! Beany locked glances with Ofila who said with a regal lift of chin, "In Acapulco when my uncle gave parties, I always sit at the table to hand peoples cup of coffee." And one of the Marias said almost pleadingly, "She wore her yellow dress to look pretty with the yellow flowers on the table."

Already Ofila was moving to the chair behind the coffee urn. She sat down, giving Beany a look of triumph.

Beany stood in helpless fury. It was no time for a scene—a scene which might well entail the bodily ousting of Ofila. Not when the mothers were already coming up the stairs for refreshments, and for meeting the new assistant at Lilac Way.

Beany could only flare out, "All right this time, Ofila. But the next time you can darn well take your turn washing dishes with the rest of the girls."

Losing her temper hadn't helped any, either.

Beany stood on in the hall, gently tugging at Red's broad ears, and thought again of Carlton's cold remark about Miss Joanne—"I told her we needed an assistant who was adult enough to handle someone like Ofila."

Dulcie Lungaarde was not the kind to keep grievances bottled up inside her.

On Sunday evening the Malone front door was opened and banged shut with that particular gustiness that proclaimed Dulcie, even before she called through the house, "Anybody home?"

"Upstairs," Beany called back. "On Mary Fred's porch."

Mary Fred, who was not at all adept in finding room on her head for curlers, was most adept at giving manicures. She had just given Adair one, and was now working on Beany.

The three Malone womenfolks looked up as Dulcie, in carhop togs, came in. "Here are some paper plates, Beany."

Beany gestured her thanks with the hand Mary Fred was not busy on. "Swell, Dulcie. Dressing for a date? Norbett again?"

"No, no date. And not with Norbett—ever. Anybody as wants him can have him."

"Don't look at me," Mary Fred said. "I told Norbett years ago to eat more carrots to improve his disposition."

"Don't look at me," Beany said. "I nursed Norbett through the *unwanted* phase of his life. Did you two have a fight?"

"No. Norbett's ashamed of me."

"Oh, now, Dulcie—"

"Wait till I tell you before you oh-now-Dulcie me. Norbett goes with this little gang of fellows and girls from college—"

"I know that clique on the campus," Mary Fred said as she guided one of Beany's hands into a bowl of soapy water. "The fellows are what one of the profs called the sneerers. They're *agin* everything."

"Where did you and Norbett go on your date?" Beany asked.

"We joined his gang at that basement café where the walls are covered with blobby pictures. Their idea of a gay, mad time is to sit around and drink this strong filtered coffee and yack-yack about how the world is going to pot. I was certainly no addition to all their talk about books and plays. And then, do you know what Norbett said to me when we left?"

"What?" Beany asked.

"He said, 'Did you have to brag about being a carhop and the tips you make?' "

"That figures," Mary Fred said. "Norbett likes to talk about the downtrodden, but he's got a streak of snobbery a yard wide."

Dulcie slumped unhappily against the doorway, and muttered, "I've run into it before. These college boys that date me—they always take me out to some little roadside joint. You don't catch them taking me to their fraternity firesides or spring formals or home-comings. Or introducing me to their sisters."

She lifted her clouded blue eyes to Adair and asked bluntly, "It's because I'm a carhop, isn't it?"

Adair answered honestly, "Yes, Dulcie, you might as well face it—it is. To your real friends it doesn't matter.

. . . But you don't have to stay a carhop. You can set yourself a goal and work toward—"

"It's easy for some," Dulcie countered. "Like you, Adair, you're a gifted artist."

Adair laughed ruefully. "Oh, no, honey. No one falls into painting portraits. It was a long, long drag. After I took all the art I could at the university, I taught it three years, and pinched and saved so I could go to Paris and Rome and study under good men there. My money didn't last. I did all sorts of odd jobs in Rome—interpreting, mopping out picture galleries, waiting tables. I'll never forget that cold, clammy winter when my shoes wore through and I'd sneak cardboard menus from the dining room to put in them. Those cold marble floors in museums. I got chilblains. But it was worth it. . . . Do you know what you want out of life, Dulcie?"

She shook her head disconsolately. "I'm not very smart."

Beany said, "Dulcie, remember that very first evening you came here? You said you wanted to be a dress designer. And you could be. Just look at how the formals you made in sewing were always the *pièce de résistance* in the Harkness style shows."

"And just think of how in the years to come," Mary Fred encouraged, "we could go to one of these swanky fashion shows, and the MC would announce, 'Now here is a charmer by Dulcie of Denver called Serenade.' "

"Pfuf! I'm a long way from there," grumbled Dulcie of Denver.

"That's right," Adair agreed. "You'd need to finish high school and go on to college. You'd need years of studying the human figure—and textiles—and color combinations."

Dulcie said, "Right now, I need to get back to the Ragged Robin before the boss does. He went home, as usual, to feed his ulcer." But she turned back to say, "Norbett never said a word about my new outfit. Come to think of it, nobody else did either. Not one of those girls sitting around looking bored in their dishwater sweaters. Except me, of course. I had to brag that even with zipper, thread, and tax, my dress only cost two-eighty-one."

12

THE days that followed the Mothers' Club meeting fell into a certain pattern. Each noontime Mrs. Harper and Beany ate lunch together in the upstairs clubroom. On the days when Miss Kunitani stayed at the pool until evening, she joined them, looking very Oriental and much more feminine in the high-necked Mandarin robe she slipped over her swim suit.

And just for the brief time of eating lunch and drinking tea with them, she unknotted the leather thong she wore around her neck with a whistle on it, and took off the diamond ring she also kept on the thong for safekeeping when she was in the water. She slid it pridefully on her finger. Her fiancé was a Japanese boy in the U.S. Navy, now stationed in Hawaii.

Sometimes Carlton Buell and the young law student, Magee, who coached the Bombshells, joined them for a cup of tea.

And sometimes one of them would comment, "Pretty gamy smell blowing from the stockyards today." But Beany was getting used to it.

Every morning the bandaged three, Violetta, Vince, and Freddy, waited for Beany on the steps. "The moulting pigeons," Carlton called them.

By now the Ho Ho's had emerged as separate personalities to Beany. Julia Veraldi was the prettiest, the friendliest, the talkingest. The unruffled Elena Zakowski and Winnie were the two most dependable and willing.

By now Beany had no trouble distinguishing the two Marias. There was the grim-eyed one who was on Juvenile Court probation for her attack on a neighbor boy. "With a broken bicycle sprocket," the young reporter-at-large had told Beany. "This boy borrowed Maria's brother's bicycle and brought it back all broke, and Maria kept hitting him with the sprocket until the police came."

The other Maria was gentle, devout. Each day in leaving, she turned at the head of the stairs to say, "Good-by, Miss Beany. I will see you tomorrow if God wants."

The gigglers—Sherry and Pam—Beany still lumped as one. Their bubbling laughter announced their coming and was the last thing she heard when the door closed behind them.

Martita, Rosa, and Dolores were the three who were always amiable, always willing, but who couldn't make a potholder in sewing, or light the oven in cooking unless Beany told them how to.

Martie Malone's near namesake was the slowest in moving her great bulky body. Life was no problem for Marcie Malone. It didn't bother her that she was seventeen and still in junior high. "I aim to get myself married pretty soon," she said comfortably.

Beverly, the girl with *café au lait* skin and sad eyes, remained an enigma. There was no drawing her out. She spoke only when she was spoken to and then in monosyllables.

Lunchtimes were usually delayed on Wednesdays.

Every Wednesday morning, Lilac Way was given over to the Baby Clinic. The recreation room, cleared of Mrs. Harper's small workers, became a waiting room. A doctor and two nurses who wore the V.N.A. arm band (Visiting Nurses' Association) took over Carlton's office. A volunteer Junior Leaguer weighed the babies in.

Beany's Wednesday morning role was that of keeping confusion and noise at a minimum. She allayed the fears

146

of foreign mothers about typhoid and diphtheria shots. She took a fretting baby out of its mother's weary arms when the waiting was overlong.

Many small children accompanied the mothers who brought their babies. These restless ones Beany took out on the grounds to a graying, motherly woman who volunteered her storytelling talent each Wednesday morning. Eugene, with his foolish smile, was one of her most avid listeners, although Violetta reported to Beany, "I have to sit by him and say, 'Now is not the time to laugh—not when the wolf eats the little pigs.' "

The days were full of surprises for Beany, too.

One noon when she was eating lunch, one of her "moulting pigeons," Freddy, came up the stairs to say, "Today is my dad's day off at the brickyard. He is here to see you, Miss Beany."

Beany's memory flitted back to her first confusing day at Lilac Way when she had taken Freddy home, and his father had bellowed out near threats about the accident. She descended the stairs in trepidation.

But the big man waiting at the foot of the stairs gave her a wide, halfway foolish smile. He was dressed quite nattily, and brick dust was barely visible in his eyebrows. He handed her a damp and heavy package. "Thought I'd bring you a little clay from the brickyards. Thought

147

maybe you could use it—you know, to make bowls and things like that down here."

"Well, yes—yes, we were thinking of doing some clay modeling. Some of the girls that don't have anything to sew—why, yes," Beany stammered in surprise. "That's so nice of you, Mr.—"

"Quinlan," he supplied. He stood on, fingering his gray hat. "I guess you found me pretty nasty-tempered that time you brought Freddy home. You caught me at a bad time. When I work on the night shift and then try to get some sleep—it's hard for me to sleep in the daytime—To tell the truth, Miss, I just naturally hate the world until I get a couple cups of coffee down me."

Beany laughed. "I know. My stepmother is the same way. She always says, 'Don't expect me to be human till I have my coffee.'"

That afternoon Beany set up a clay-modeling table for the Ho Ho's who had no material for sewing. Drawing from her own scanty experience, she showed them how to make ropes of clay for building up bowls or ash trays. And here the withdrawn, unresponsive, untalkative Beverly surprised Beany.

Beverly's hands could turn a lump of clay into something animate. At the end of the session she had a figure of a small girl who was looking down at her feet.

"What is she so happy about?" Beany asked.

148

"That is my little sister," Beverly said, "when her dad brought her white shoes. It was her first pair of new shoes. He won the money in a crap game."

One of the girls asked, "Did he bring you a pair, too?"

"He is not my father," Beverly said in her expressionless voice.

Beany looked puzzled, and Marcie Malone explained, "Beverly's got three sisters, but they've all got different fathers."

Beany thought soberly, I guess this is what is known as finding out how the other half lives.

As the June days flitted by, all attention at Lilac Way focused on the Fourth of July. The Bombshells would play their first official game in the Young America series. For it, Mrs. Harper's artists were making water-color and crayon posters for display in stores and barbershops.

Beany's Ho Ho's were making a banner to hang over the Bombshell dugout. On a wide canvas, donated by Bartell Bottling, they were stitching green letters—BOMBSHELLS.

And where did the green felt come from? The summer before when Mary Fred worked at the dude ranch, she had worn a skirt of bright green felt. Beany reminded her that she wasn't wearing it now—and it was just the right green. . . .

"Our Beany's turned into a worse scavenger than Father Hugh," Mary Fred sighed as she handed it to her. "It's getting so I have to hide my clothes under the pillow when I take them off at night."

There was another chore the Ho Ho sewers did with even greater zeal. On the Fourth of July, Ofila would take part in the city high-diving meet. She brought to Lilac Way another swim suit of flame-colored satin which was less faded than the one she practiced in. It, too, was spangled, but Ofila wanted even more spangles on it.

"But, Ofila," Beany suggested, "the other girl contestants won't be wearing suits with beads on them."

Again that look of lofty disdain. "What the others wear, I do not care. In the paper last year I was call the diving flame. This year I will be call the same."

The Ho Ho's vied with each other in sewing crystal beads from the dime store on it.

The community center tennis tournament also got under way on the Fourth. Winnie, who had easily won the tryouts—as everyone knew she would—was to represent Lilac Way.

The day before she said shyly, "If you aren't too busy. Miss Beany, I would like you to come and watch me play."

"I'll be there rooting for you," Beany promised.

And Angelo Veraldi of the sticky fingers and roguish smile said, "Hey, Miss Beany, you comin' out to see us play the Blue Tigers tomorrow?"

Violetta put in earnestly, "I have already burned four candles and said prayers—"

"Mr. Bull told you to keep off your sore knee, Violetta," Beany reminded her.

"I only kneeled on one knee long enough to pray that the Bombshells beat the hell out of the Blue Tigers."

Ofila did *not* invite Miss Beany to be present at the diving meet. But she heard her tell Carlton, "Meestaire Buell, I am what you say—superstitious. If you are not there to see, I cannot dive so high in the air or go into the water with only the very little splash."

"I'll get out there for the finish anyway," he promised.

On the morning of the fifth when Beany entered the clubroom, a new diving trophy sat on the sideboard. Ofila, with willing help from admiring Ho Ho's, was tacking up more pictures, more write-ups. Rave write-ups from both the *Call* and *Tribune!* (The *Tribune* one was *not* by Norbett Rhodes.)

Again the reporter likened Señorita Gonzales to a flame as, in mid-air, the sun caught her shimmering red suit. And perhaps because of the very unusualness of it, he made a point of the earrings and bracelets which were as much a part of her exotic charm as her smoldering "black eyes."

Beany wished he hadn't played up the jewelry. It irritated her the way all the Ho Ho's copied Ofila and wore cheap, dangly earrings and wide, ornate bracelets.

The reporter had even made a heroine out of the *señorita* from Acapulco. He said that in climbing the tower she had slipped and hurt her elbow, but had only shrugged and would not stop to have it dressed.

Violetta, who was perhaps a little jealous that it was now Ofila who waited for Mr. Bull to "banditch" her elbow, said, "It will soon be well. It is only a scratch. And elbows get better sooner than knees, because you do not kneel on elbows."

In the same papers the sports section gave scanty space to "Bombshells Defeated by Blue Tigers." And still scantier to Winnie Pickett of Lilac Way scoring a victory over her opponent in the community center tennis tournament.

"It was like that last year," Violetta said. "She beat everybody till she played that awful tall girl from Carter Center with arms long as bed slats."

These were busy days for Mr. Bull with all the summer activities gathering momentum. With the bare-bones budget to watch.

But for Beany's Ho Ho's there came a lethargic slump.

They had worked with diligent enthusiasm to meet the deadline of the Mothers' Club meeting. For the Fourth of July events, they had fashioned the Bombshell banner, tinseled Ofila's suit, made cake and ice cream for the team when they returned to Lilac Way. Now there was no goal to aim for. The sewing machines ran halfheartedly in the making of bean bags for Mrs. Harper's kindergarten group.

Their boredom and edginess seemed to reach a peak on a sultry July afternoon. The fighting Maria had an ugly gleam in her eye because her pottery bowl had cracked in the dry heat. Even the clay figure Beverly shaped looked bowed and desolate. Maybe it would be just as well to dismiss the class early to go into the pool.

Beany always found some excuse for not going in. She was ashamed to have her pupils and Miss Kunitani see that she couldn't make a decent dive off the board or from the side. She regretted now that she hadn't stayed with Junior Lifesaving at Harkness High.

She heard male footsteps ascending the stairs, and got to her feet in surprise to see Father Hugh and Andy Kern.

The small scramble of introductions, of giving them chairs, of asking, "How about a cold drink?" and Father

Hugh lifting a tufted eyebrow and snorting, "None of that sweet slop, but I would like some coffee."

Elena Zakowski got to her feet with an "I'll have some right away," and the next second Beany heard the rattle of percolator in the kitchen, and the puff of gas flame going on under it.

Andy said, "This is my day off, and I was running errands for Father Hugh. He wanted me to bring him down to look you all over."

"I wanted to see if mayhaps in all the junk I'm forever collecting, I had something you could use." The priest's keen eyes raked over the Ho Ho's. "Could you make use of some of these bandana handkerchiefs—sure, each one is big as a lunchcloth?"

Beany nodded. "We certainly could, I think."

"Andy, go down and bring those up—I'll not be climbing the stairs again. Run along with him, a few of you. They're in great bales."

They all flocked down, except Elena Zakowski, who stood over the coffeepot, and Beverly, who was wetting cloths to wrap her clay figure in.

The bales of red and blue bandanas filled three chairs. "Wherever did you get them, Father Hugh?" Beany asked.

"Never mind, never mind, that's a trade secret."

"Maybe a store had them for years and couldn't sell them," ventured Violetta. "Because they are very big just to blow a nose on."

Father Hugh gave her his quizzical smile. "And maybe a roof leaked and a trickle of water seeped onto them leaving a watery spot here and there. But as the Irish say, 'Sure, it'll never show on a gallopin' horse.' "

Father Hugh drank the coffee Elena set before him, and visited with them all on their own level, scolding to some, tender to others. A loving, blunt-spoken man.

He leaned over for a closer look at Ofila's blouse—one of her white fiesta ones that Beany had felt an itch to dip in suds. "That's a pretty thing, but you're not washing it right. I've got some sample soap powder—detergent, I guess they call it—that's guaranteed to whiten without fading colors. I'll send you a package."

Beany expected Ofila to stiffen and make a cold reply. Instead she said, *"Gracias, Padre.* My great-aunt has only soap in the brick."

He turned his eyes on the statue Beverly was blanketing in wet cloths. "Let's see that now. What is the poor woman so sad about?"

The Negro girl said simply, "It is my mother the day the telegram came that my brother was killed in Korea. I was a little girl but I remember how she sat like that."

"Ah, yes—yes. The grief of a mother. Have you other brothers?"

"No, Father. Only girls. Our mother does not care for us the way she did Ronnie that was killed."

"Well now, there's nothing the matter with girls. Well—now—" The way he said it made Beany sure that Father Hugh might find time to seek out Beverly's mother and have a little talk with her.

The Ho Ho's basked in the presence of their male visitors. The gigglers giggled the harder when Andy asked, "What are you two so sober about?" and Father Hugh said, "Ah, laugh while you can. The day will come when you'll think you'll never laugh again."

And when they rose to leave, Andy said, "Hey, Knucks—I mean, Miss Beany, how about my swinging by and taking you home? I thought you might even limber up your fryin' arm and ask me to dinner."

"I'll start limberin'," Beany said.

It was the gigglers who asked it before Andy and Father Hugh were out the front door. "Is Andy your beau?"

"Yes, he's been my beau for quite a while. Let's see how many bandanas there are. Would you like to make skirts out of them?"

Would they! They pulled them in disarray, trying them for width and length. Ofila was as elated as the others. Beany could scarcely believe her ears when Ofila said, "You have the swell idea, Miss Beany, to make skirts out of these so big handkerchiefs."

Elena Zakowski counted them. Four dozen in each of the four bales. "We'll have enough to make sleeveless blouses, too," she said.

Beany thought back to a year ago when the Malones had held a festive outdoor supper for which she and her friends had frantically stitched up fiesta skirts and blouses. She said impulsively, "After we've all made ourselves bandana skirts and blouses, why don't we have a midsummer party? A real fancy cookout party here on the grounds?"

They considered that with only a small spurt of enthusiasm. Marcie Malone summed it up with a grumbled, "Ain't much fun having a party just for ourselves. It's ourselves we're tired of being with."

No, an all-girl party was at best a tame affair, Beany realized. She said on a bold inspiration, "I'll tell you! Let's ask the Hikers."

There was no chorus of "Yes, let's!" The girls squirmed in shy unease. The gigglers tittered. Animosity flashed in the fighting Maria's eyes. Heavens, could the boy she had whacked with the broken bicycle sprocket be one of the Hikers? Ofila sat in frozen dignity.

Beany could understand their lack of response. She had asked Carlton once, "How come your Hikers stick close to each other when they're at Lilac Way, and my Ho Ho's knot up solid, and there's no fraternizing? The age brackets are right. The nationalities just about match. What ails your Hikers?"

Carlton's grin was rueful. "About half of them are at the girl-shy stage. And the other half consider themselves such wolves—you know, the kind that stand on the corner and whistle as the girls go by—that the Ho Ho's aren't flashy enough for them."

"We ought to do something about it."

"If you can think up something, you have my blessing," Carlton said.

Marcie Malone was summing it up for Beany from the Ho Ho's viewpoint. "Them Hikers think they're pretty much. They make fun of us, Miss Beany. All except Waldo. He ain't as uppity as the others."

Beany remembered Waldo, a lanky Negro boy who had been swiftly eliminated in the tennis tryouts.

"Oh, no, they don't! I'll bet they'd be tickled to death to come to your cookout," she reassured them. "Let's do it up in style. I'll invite Andy, and we'll ask Mr. Buell—and how about Miss Cirisi?"

158

"Every summer Miss Cirisi goes to a party at Carter Center," the amiable Martita said. "I know because my cousin told me so."

"Then we'll ask her, too," Beany said.

Her very enthusiasm carried them along. They consulted a calendar and set the day—a week from the coming Saturday which would give them time to make their bandana skirts and blouses. They penned the invitation which read formally, "The Ho Ho Club cordially invites the Hikers—"

Elena Zakowski was to take it home to her brother Oleg, who would pass it on to his brother Hikers.

The fighting Maria said, "Be just like them to eat our food and then walk off."

"Of course they won't," Beany encouraged. She looked again at the calendar. "We can sit around the fire and sing songs because there'll be a full moon that night."

"If God wills," murmured the pious Maria.

Marcie Malone said, "Yeah, Waldo can bring his guitar if his old lady hasn't hocked it to buy herself gin."

It wasn't until Beany had completely sold the idea to the others that she began to have misgivings herself.

She told Andy Kern about it as she rode home from Lilac Way with him that evening. She told him what

Carlton had said about some of the Hikers being too girl-shy, and some not girl-shy enough.

"Goodness, Andy, do you suppose I've bitten off more than I can chew?"

He chuckled, and nudged her as he drove, "Old Andy will be there. He'll help you chew."

13

THE Hikers accepted the Ho Ho's invitation with pleasure.

On Friday afternoon, a week and a day before the party, sewing machines and tongues were clattering merrily in the clubroom when Elena Zakowski arrived. She was late, she explained, because Mrs. Morrison, her employer, had kept her with extra work for an anniversary party the Morrisons were having that night.

Elena was wearing a wide silver bracelet with turquoise stones, and the girls gathered about to admire it and ask where she got it. Elena was uneasily evasive. Yes, it was a—sort of present. "I won't wear it every day. I just wore it to show it to you."

So even the sensible Elena was not immune to the earring-bracelet influence of Ofila! The dangling earrings and wide bracelets had shown up even more since the reporter had described Ofila's so glowingly—"As much a part of her exotic charm as her smoldering black eyes."

Again the talk turned to the menu for their cookout. The girls were to divide the cost among themselves. Again they decided that it must, of economic necessity, be hamburgers. It wasn't that they didn't like hamburgers, but they would have liked something more *partyish* and impressive.

They brightened when Beany told them of her plan for the dessert. Mary Fred, who was often at the Carmody farm to ride and keep an eye on old Charlie's tippling, had reported to Beany that a cherry tree was beginning to ripen.

"I remember last year they were ready about the middle of July," Beany said. "So how about cherry tarts? And we can get thick cream to whip, too."

And could they all go out to pick them? they asked on squeals of excitement.

"Yes, we'll go out the day before."

Again the absent Carmodys were providing for Beany's Ho Ho's. But if they were home, she realized, the generous Miggs and her mother would probably insist on donating the pastry shells to go with the cherries as well.

Elena left her stitching of her skirt to measure Marcie Malone. "It'll take a lot of them bandanas to go around me," Marcie admitted with her comfortable laugh.

The afternoon was well along when a step sounded on the stairs. Every girl stiffened as though some inner alarm were sounded that this was an alien step.

And so it was. A policeman in summer uniform of navy-blue shirt and pants, and holster belt sagging with its weight of gun, came to the doorway. He touched his cap as Beany walked toward him. "I'm Sergeant Haynes, Miss. I'm looking for—" he consulted a paper, "—Elena Zakowski. Which one is she?"

Beany looked back at the class. Elena stood, her eyes wide in her paper-gray face, clutching a wad of bandanas to her.

"Elena, come here a minute," Beany said.

One of the girls took the handkerchiefs out of her hand as she passed. The fighting Maria said out of the corner of her mouth, "Don't you tell him nothin', kid."

The policeman wasted no words. "Did you swipe a bracelet from that Mrs. Morrison you work for?"

Elena's blue eyes dropped guiltily to her wrist. The officer lifted her hand and looked at the jewelry. "That's it you're wearing, huh?"

No sound came from Elena's parted lips, and the officer consulted the paper again. "Silver. Large turquoise in center—two smaller. I guess you'd better come with me."

Beany gasped, "Oh, Elena! You didn't take that bracelet from Mrs. Morrison, did you?"

Elena wrenched it off, thrust it at Beany. "I wasn't going to steal it. I was just going to wear it down here and show the girls, and then I was going to take it back in the morning when I did her ironing."

"You'll have to come with me," Sergeant Haynes said.

"I'll go with you," Beany said. "I'll talk to Mrs. Morrison and tell her you didn't mean to steal it."

The three walked down the steps together, climbed into the black roadster Sergeant Haynes was driving. They sat in rigid silence all the way to the Morrison ranch-style house in a suburb near the airport.

Mrs. Morrison flung open the door for them, flustered and defensive and voluble, while her two little girls sat silently on the couch. "Yes, that's it—that's it," she said when Beany held the bracelet out to her. "My husband got it for me on our honeymoon—and so I always wear it on our anniversary. And today I went to get it—and I couldn't believe my eyes when it wasn't right there in the box where I always keep it. And then Kitty—she's my little girl—said she saw Lena trying it on. I wouldn't have anything happen to it for

164

anything—those are real turquoises—and besides it's the sentiment—"

Beany got her word in. "She didn't mean to steal it, Mrs. Morrison. She only meant to borrow it and bring it back the first thing in the morning."

"How do I know she did? That's what she says. I mean, everyone says you can never tell about girls that come from that part of town—"

The policeman asked, "You want to prefer charges against her?"

"Well—I don't know—"

"Please don't," Beany pleaded. "Elena isn't the kind to—"

"You got your jewelry back," Sergeant Haynes said and, for the first time, showed that he had a heart under his heat-wrinkled blue shirt. "Once you file charges it's always on the record against her."

"All right, then I won't. I just wish it hadn't happened. I liked having Lena here—she's a good worker and the children liked her—but you can see I can't have her come back. I'll send you your money, Lena."

Elena only nodded in stricken silence. She didn't say a word, not even when the small girls clutched at her, crying that they didn't want her to go. She gently loosened their grasp. Beany took her arm, and they followed the policeman back to the car. Again there seemed nothing to say on the drive back.

They reached the part of town where the familiar stockyards smell was in the air, and Beany said, "You turn here, Sergeant Haynes, to go to Lilac Way."

He didn't turn. "I'm taking her home. I went there first, and her old man told me to bring her back after I took her to see Mrs. Morrison."

He stopped in front of a small white house with a white picket fence. Beany had pictured Elena living in just such a tidy house with flowers and well-tended shrubbery around it.

The man of the house was standing at the gate waiting. Beany's first impression was that he was a short, neat, and kindly man, and she waited to catch his eyes to explain the whole unfortunate affair.

He gave her not so much as a glance. He opened the gate for Elena who slid through, and asked her, "Did you steal from that woman?"

Beany pushed inside the gate and said swiftly, "But she only meant to borrow it, and the woman was real nice and isn't going to do anything about it."

He gave Beany a dismissing glance, and again asked his daughter, "You stole from her?"

Elena nodded.

The man reached in his pocket, drew out a knife, pried out the blade, and walked to a bushy tree that hung over the fence. Beany watched in unbelieving horror as he cut a branch, neatly trimmed off the twigs.

"Come," he said to Elena.

Beany turned her eyes to the mother standing on the porch steps—the nice-mannered woman who had come to the Mothers' Club. Wasn't she going to interfere? The younger children on the porch watched with faces that held no expression. Beany looked at Elena, expecting to see horror or fear or rebellion in her flowerlike face. There was only acceptance.

Beany laid a hand on Mr. Zakowski's stocky arm. "Don't whip her," she cried. "She was only going to show the bracelet to the girls, and then in the morning—"

He removed her arm and said with dignity, "Young lady, I do not raise thieves."

And Elena looked back over her shoulder to say, "It's all right, Miss Beany. I shouldn't have taken the bracelet."

The door closed behind Elena and her father, leaving Beany standing at the gate. Sergeant Haynes called to her from the car, "Come on, Miss, and I'll take you back to the center."

She was shaking as she climbed in beside him, and he drove off. "*You're* the police," she accused him shrilly. "Couldn't you have stopped him?"

"No, I couldn't. And maybe I didn't want to. Say what you want about these old country fathers, it's not their kids that fill up Juvenile Court and reform schools."

It was past time for the Ho Ho's sewing class, but they still waited for Beany in the clubroom, their hands idle. "What'd they do to Elena?" one asked tensely; and another, "Is that woman going to file charges against her?"

How well they knew the machinery of the law!

"No, she isn't. She fired her, of course. But her father was waiting—and he cut a big switch off a tree—and he—"

She dropped her head on the sewing machine where Elena's bandana skirt was in the making, and sobbed.

They circled around her, trying awkwardly to comfort her. She said thickly, "It's time for you to go, girls."

Marcie Malone said in leave-taking, "Don't you cry about it, Miss Beany. I've been whipped lots of times. It ain't so bad—just while it lasts."

At last Beany was alone, except for Violetta and Vince who sat gravely silent for once. They watched as Beany, in a sudden frenzy of activity, ran the machine and stitched together blue bandanas for Elena's skirt. At least she could do that for her.

She was still at the machine when Carlton called up the stairs to ask her to come down to the office. She thought he wanted to talk about the Zakowski affair, and she poured it all out to him.

He listened soberly. "I know it seems terrible to you, Beany. Things like that did to me, too, when I first started down here. Now—well, maybe I'm a little like your policeman. The kids to feel sorry for are the ones that have parents that don't bother their heads about them."

It was clear Carlton had something else on his mind, for, after a brief silence, he asked abruptly, "How good a swimmer are you, Beany?"

"I'm not what you'd call Olympic material. You see, I—"

"How much lifesaving training have you had?"

"I was in the group at Harkness my junior year and I got along O.K. except for diving. When I had a chance to get on the school paper, all that underwater-approach stuff seemed kind of futile. Why, Carl?"

"We've got to do some juggling around here at Lilac Way. Miss Kunitani is quitting to get married and—"

"But her fiancé is in Hawaii."

"He's getting a leave, and she's going to meet him in San Francisco. She and her mother are leaving two weeks from today. So we've got to have a worker here that can teach the children's classes in the morning, and guard the pool two weekday afternoons when Coach Magee has baseball practice, and on Saturdays when the games are played. He'll take over the rest of the time."

"But I'd have to pass the Red Cross lifesaving test first, wouldn't I?"

He nodded. "You couldn't even teach kids in shallow water without the Water Safety Instructor emblem."

Beany remembered the skill she had seen Miss Kunitani demonstrate that first day. Into the water like an arrow, hooking her arm around the panicky swimmer—Beany remembered her biggest stumbling block when she took lifesaving was diving. And then she thought of the person whose black hair was seldom dry. . . .

"Carl, couldn't Ofila fill in? She's a regular fish in the water."

"No. Miss Cirisi and I talked it over and decided she wouldn't do."

"Because she's a Mexican?"

"Good heavens, no. There's no color or race line in recreation center work. Because she's no good at teaching. I asked her to give Kunitani a hand once. She's cross and impatient with the kids."

Carlton had very evidently been thinking of Beany as taking Miss Kunitani's place and had already done some groundwork for it. "The timing isn't so bad. An Admiral Blesek is the only man in this region qualified to give the lifesaving test. I got hold of him, and he tells me he's slated to give one two weeks from tomorrow at the Y. You've—we've—a lot to crowd in, in that time."

"I'm a lousy diver," she put in.

He passed over that remark. "But I've seen it done when there's an emergency like this. I took the lifesaving test from this same Admiral Blesek when I was sixteen. It's no snap but—"

"It's either pass it or be out of a job, isn't it?" she asked bluntly.

"I'm afraid so, Beany. Miss Cirisi and I would hate to see you go. But it's late in the season to pick up a part-time lifeguard."

She sat and listened almost dully to Carlton's outlining of plans. His uncle, Matthew Buell, had a good-sized pool at his home in the suburbs. No one was using it, because Uncle Matt was staying at a downtown club while his wife and daughter were away. Only a caretaker was there looking after the grounds and pool.

171

"Uncle Matt's married daughter takes her little boy there once in a while. So we could go ahead full steam on drilling you for the test," he added.

Beany's heart was thumping in uneasy fright. This would be for real, not something she had taken for a credit at school with no thought of ever practicing.

Carlton stood up. "We can get started this evening. I'll take you home and you get your suit. Eat a light supper, and we'll set out for Uncle Matt's pool. The evenings are long. We can get up early in the mornings and work for a few hours too. It'll be a tough grind, but—What do you say, Beany?"

She wanted to say, "No. No, I'm not the athletic type." But it was either, or.

It wasn't only the salary she would need this fall. It was that if she dropped out of Lilac Way now, she would leave so much *unfinished*. The Ho Ho's and their rosy plans for the party—and after all, Beany had egged them into it. And Elena. Beany had to be on hand to comfort her when she came back to the clubrooms, crushed and cowed.

Her eyes dropped to the wilted tuberous begonia on her blouse Eugene had given her that morning, and about which Violetta had pondered long. "I wonder what grave he got that off of. It must be somebody new." She thought of her moulting pigeons who always

172

waited on the steps for her. She even thought of Ofila with a glow of warmth and pride. Ofila *was* adjusting happily. She had been downright friendly to Beany lately.

She got up from the sagging sofa and said, though a little shakily, "I'll do my durnedest, Carl."

14

AFTERWARDS Beany was to remember the very time and place when Carlton changed from being good old Carl next door and became Mr. Bull, director of Lilac Way.

The time was that same Friday evening when the sun was still high in the sky. The place was the Matthew Buell swimming pool with its setting of lawn and shrubs, all enclosed in a high fence of cedar poles, the gate of which the caretaker Gallagher had opened for them.

As Beany dropped down on the edge of the pool and started to put her feet into waist-high water, he ordered, "No, Beany. Might as well learn right now to go in head-first. It's always a dead giveway that a person is no expert when he wades into the water."

"I was never good at diving," she told him again.

"You've *got* to do a standing dive and a running dive from the edge of the pool."

He stood beside her, showed her how to point her hands over her head. "See that leaf floating on the water there? Say to yourself, 'I'll hit that with my hands and then my head—and then my feet.' "

Thus ordered, Beany went in. But neither her hands nor her head hit the leaf. Her middle did, and received a vicious slap from the water. And when she thrashed about, gasping and snuffling in water, her teacher wasted no sympathy on her.

"You know better than to breathe through your nose in the water. The minute you come to the surface, blow *out* through your nose, and open your mouth for a big bite of air. Try it again. Bow your back and push with your feet. Like this."

He did it effortlessly. She tried seven times before she did a dive from the edge that was even creditable.

Carlton motioned to her. "We'll start working on your crawl. Remember the day Kunitani brought the boy out of deep water? She used the crawl after her distance dive, and reached him in about three good strokes. Watch."

Down went Carlton's crewcut head into the water. One, two, three strokes—the face was lifted sideways on the third for a mouthful of air.

175

Beany's "flutter" with her feet wasn't right—not for a lifesaver.

He drilled her without mercy—this businesslike Mr. Bull who seemed to think she had more strength in her arms and legs, more wind under her ribs than she had.

The sun slid all the way down behind the poplars, down behind the mountain peaks. Carlton still swam beside her in the dusk, a tireless robot with pistons for arms. "Reach farther on your strokes. Cup your hands. You don't get a *pull* when your fingers are spread."

At last he called quits. Beany's eyes were bleary. Her flesh smarted from her flat dives. She had no strength left to dress, but slid wet feet into sandals, and pulled her blouse over her shoulders. Her hair was matted to her head, but she was too tired to run a comb through it.

Mr. Bull said as they walked to his station wagon, "We've got a lot of ground—or water—to cover in two weeks."

Thus began the most rigorous, most ruthless drilling Beany had ever known. The next morning at five, he wakened her by opening the front door and saying to Red, "Go get Beany up." Carlton gave her his Red Cross book, *Lifesaving and Water Safety,* to study. He constantly quoted Admiral Blesek.

On Monday morning she and Carlton reached Lilac Way after a three-hour workout in the pool. Violetta was on hand to report that Uncle Benny was *in* again, and that the traveling pain of Ofila's great-aunt was now behind her ear. She added, "Miss Beany, Winnie wants you to serve her real fast balls."

"Gosh, Carl, my muscles are too sore to lift a tennis racket."

"Better to keep them limbered up. Go ahead and practice with Winnie." That was Mr. Bull talking.

And it was Mr. Bull who called to her as she left the tennis court, limp and panting, a half-hour later. "Come here and watch Ofila a minute." He called across to the girl in the red swim suit, "Do a jack next."

Beany steadied herself by a hold on the mesh fence, and watched the slim figure leap high off the board, fold up until the finger tips touched her ankles; watched the legs straighten and pointed toes disappear into the water.

"Now, that's the technique to use for your surface dive, Beany. Throw yourself up out of the water, and then straight down as though you were trying to grab your ankles."

Beany had gone through a bad time the day before on a surface dive to bring up the whistle Carlton dropped on the bottom of the pool. "Admiral Blesek will have you bring up a weight," he told her.

The very urgency of this lifesaving test pushed everything else to second place in Beany's mind. Even the plans for the Ho Ho's cookout.

On this same Monday afternoon, Mr. Bull came up to the clubroom and asked, "Now, what menu are you girls planning for your party Saturday night?"

Hamburgers, they told him. Anything else cost too much.

"How many of you know how to dress a chicken?"

A titter from the gigglers. "You mean pull the feathers off and the—the insides out?"

Marcie Malone turned on them in scorn. "What'd you think *dressing* a chicken means? Putting on a hat and coat? I sure can dress chickens, Mr. Bull."

Four or five others admitted to being chicken dressers. *Not* Ofila, of course.

Carlton told them about his farmer friend who had more roosters than he wanted to keep, and would sell them for twenty-five cents each undressed. "That way a half-chicken won't cost a cent more than hamburger. How about my telling the farmer to bring them in Friday afternoon?"

The titter from the gigglers, who wanted to know if the chickens would be dead or alive, was drowned out by the delighted chorus of, "It'll be swell to have chicken for

178

our party," and Marcie Malone's, "If he wants to bring them with the heads on, I can bring a hatchet."

The heads would be off, Mr. Bull told them.

That same Monday evening Andy Kern telephoned Beany and led off with a scolding, "Didn't Mary Fred tell you I called yesterday and that I wanted you to call me back? At home?"

"She told me, Andy. Don't be mad at me. I was so beat when I got back from swimming, I went to sleep on the couch and didn't wake up until a shooting program came on TV at ten-thirty." She told him about her need to pass the lifesaving test to keep her job at Lilac Way. "Learning tennis was just tiddlywinks compared to this."

"Right you are, Knucks. Whenever you see that W.S.I. badge on a suit, you know it's been earned. I'll all but genuflect when you get yours. What time should I appear at your cookout Saturday?"

"Seven. And not our *cookout*," she reproved primly, "it's our *barbecue*. Chicken, no less. You remember Marcie Malone? She tells us that Waldo, one of the Hikers, can eat a whole chicken without drawing a breath."

"Point Waldo out to me. So I can get ahead of him in the line."

Beany chortled. "Carl and Miss Cirisi won't be there for the supper. They have to go to a Young America banquet first."

Elena Zakowski was another of life's surprises to Beany. She told Mary Fred about it. "I thought she'd come back to Lilac Way crushed and cowed, or maybe so bitter against her father that she'd want to run away from home. But no, she came back just as serene as ever."

"I can understand that," Mary Fred mused. "It's the way she has been brought up. Papa is the judge, jury, and carrier-out of sentence. Elena felt she had it coming to her—probably felt relieved. We've got a young woman at Beth San who hates her father, and has messed up her life out of some unconscious resentment toward him. And yet *he* never laid a hand on her. He just broke her spirit and dominated her in a nice, soft-voiced way."

On Friday evening, as Carlton and Beany were returning from a tiring three hours in the pool, Mr. Bull turned back into good old Carl. Driving down College Boulevard in the dusk, their eyes were caught by the on-and-off neon sign at the Ragged Robin that told of their shrimps-in-a-boat special. "You as hungry as I am, Beany?" Carlton said. "Let's stop and have us some shrimp."

"Sounds heavenly, Carl."

Dulcie came bouncing along to take their order, and Carlton went to the telephone booth. Beany said, "Dulcie, I'm sorry. I've been intending to ask Trighorn if he fixed your purse so I could bring it back to you. But I've been so busy."

Dulcie lifted her blackened eyebrows. "Spare the apologies, mate. My coral purse is all fixed and back in circulation."

"Oh! Oh, you mean Trighorn brought it back himself?"

This time Dulcie's mascaraed eyelashes fluttered over her sparkling eyes. "There's no law against the repairman delivering, is there? And no law against his wanting to be sure the clasp held up for an evening of dancing?"

"Fine thing! I bring a man home, and he fixes Johnny's car, and your purse, and then he takes you dancing."

Dulcie was soon back with the order. She asked, "What's holding up your boy friend Carl?"

"He's phoning our respective homes to tell them not to keep our dinners warming up and drying out in the ovens."

"He's for real, that guy. I always did think you were a sap not to latch on to him before somebody else beat you to it. Why don't you?"

"Two reasons, Dulcie. One is that Carl doesn't want anyone latching on to him. Johnny always said he'd go into deep freeze if he thought a gal was warming up to him. And the other reason is that I'm halfway latched to Andy."

"Andy!" Dulcie snorted. "You're stretching a point if you think Andy's even halfway latched to you. I saw him dancing with a luscious little redhead out at Acacia Gardens."

Carlton returned then.

Beany hungrily nibbled shoestring potatoes and crisp shrimps. Funny that she felt no unhappy surge of jealousy over Dulcie's news about Andy. She must be awfully one-track-minded to let a lifesaving test crowd out all feminine emotions.

That evening opportunity came knocking at her door, and she was even too weary to open the door wide.

Her father was waiting for her when she came in. "Beany, at last there's something opening at the *Call* that could well be your toehold on a permanent job there."

One of their feature writers, he explained, was to do a series on juvenile delinquency. "The boss and I were talking about it, and I suggested that at the same time we run—as sort of counterbalance—a more hopeful picture of young people and what community centers and Young America leagues are doing for them."

"You mean *I* would write them?"

"Sure. Firsthand stuff. You've got the material right at your finger tips. Give the personal side of some of the kids on the Bombshells—your Angelo, for instance. And what the Ho Ho Club means to the teen-age girls."

Martie Malone's own face was alight. "It'd just mean putting on paper some of the stories you've told us when you come home."

"Yes," Beany agreed. "Yes, it would." But no itch came to her fingers. "Can it wait, Dad? In just a week from tomorrow, I take the lifesaving test—and I'll either be in or out at Lilac Way. Right now my whole brain feels waterlogged."

15

"Do you think it's going to rain?"

Over and over again the Ho Ho's asked it of each other and Beany when, late on Saturday afternoon, they carried out their supper supplies and built a fire in the outdoor fireplace.

They even appealed to Eugene on his bench, who was somewhat of a weather forecaster, "Do you think it'll rain, Eugene?" He studied the busily shifting clouds through his thick lenses. "After while." He smiled.

The Hikers began to arrive at a quarter of seven. Not one came alone but in groups of two or three. They were dressed for the occasion; but they were ill at ease, and formed a male lump as though their hostesses didn't exist. The girls, too, tightened their group.

Oh, dear! Maybe this idea of Beany's wasn't so good after all. Try as she would, she couldn't mix the two groups. The girls were edgy and taut.

Beany looked up with relief at sight of Andy Kern. He was wearing a big sombrero, cowboy boots, and his widest grin. It was he who enlisted the Hikers to help him weight down the tablecloth and paper plates when the wind whipped up; he who said, "Hey, men, how about giving the girls a hand with the fire? Never saw a female yet that could get a bed of coals."

But still there was no relaxed give and take between them, although Andy saw to it that, when they sat down with their platefuls, the boys didn't all sit on one side of the table. Andy loudly praised the barbecued chicken and potato salad. And, taking a cue from him, the Hikers grunted with a brief raising of eyes, "Yeah, sure is good."

The dessert had to be served hurriedly, for the wind was stronger, the sky blacker, and a few spatters of rain hissed on the fireplace coals.

Oh, dear again! No moon. No lounging about and singing to Waldo's guitar. They had no recourse but to gulp down the cherry tarts, gather up the perishables, and run for the big recreation room where Mrs. Harper had cleared the tables on which her charges made giraffes and painted posters.

At first there was all the bustle of opening folding chairs, of the boys helping to carry the silverware up to the clubrooms, of everyone clunking empty bottles back in Bartell cases.

And then the woeful silence.

The girls sat on the folding chairs against the wall, the shoulders of their bandana blouses wet with rain, and dropped their eyes to the hands in their laps. A clink or two as Ofila pushed back her hair and looked questioningly at Beany. No one had thought to send Eugene home, and he was there, too, eating chicken someone had slipped him.

The boys again formed their indissoluble lump. Beany's own voice sounded falsely bright to her ears as she said, "How about a little music?" And Marcie Malone, who seemed less daunted than the other girls, bellowed out, "You, Waldo! Did you bring your guitar like I told you?"

Only a self-conscious shuffling of feet from Waldo, and a muttered something about his being no musician.

Andy was having trouble with the record player and solicited help from the boys. And still the girls sat stiffly, and still the boys knotted together in the corner near the door.

Beany's heart dropped lower and lower. Not this leaden end to the party they had worked so hard for! All

186

that stitching together of blue and red handkerchiefs—
and dressing chickens, and picking cherries this morning
and pitting them this hot afternoon—not to mention the
making of pastry and potato salad. Oh, it had been a
mistake for her to say, "Let's have the Hikers."

They were edging closer to the door. In another
minute there would be some mumbled excuse, and they
would exit as one—rain or no.

The record player gave a loud, arresting bleat. Andy
adjusted it until rhythmic south-of-the-border music
filled the big rectangle of room. He put two fingers into
his mouth and whistled for attention. "Ladies and
gentlemen, our opening number on the program will be
the Mexican Hat Dance by Señor Andrio Kernez."

He tossed his sombrero on the floor and, with arms
on hips, began a mincing, farcical, heel-clicking dance
around it. No one could clown like Andy. The first grins
turned to guffaws from the boys and laughter from the
girls as Andy clamped one booted foot on the other and
had to reach down and pry it off.

Ofila started a shouted *"Ole! Ole!"* and others took it
up with clapping and stamping to accent the rhythm.

A time or two Andy's feet went out from under him,
and he sat on the hat he wasn't supposed to touch. The
gigglers giggled until Beany wondered they had any
breath left. And as Andy started a backward *thump-*

thump step, looking over his shoulder at the hat, the guitar magically appeared on its strap around Waldo's neck, and Waldo's long, black fingers were picking at the strings.

Andy pretended to drop in exhaustion, but Waldo kept on playing. Soon he was accompanied by a mouth harp, played by a fair-haired boy they called Dodo. By now Marcie Malone was pulling the shrinking, devout Maria to her feet and toward the piano. Maria played, while Marcie in deep-throated fervor sang, "When the Saints Come Marching In." Everyone joined in.

The party turned into a hilarious talent show. There would be laughing consultation and the shoving of someone onto the floor. Tap dancing. A take-off on Ed Sullivan. Elena and Oleg Zakowski did a Cossack dance.

Carlton and Miss Cirisi came in when the party was at its height. Miss Cirisi watched with sparkling eyes, and Carlton, who seemed tired and preoccupied, looked on with his "Bless you, my children" smile.

Ofila, after some directions to the pianist, guitar player, and mouth harpist, stood in the middle of the room to announce, "I will do the Flame Dance I was do at my uncle's where the flat rock is so very high up like a mountain. There, I do it with torches in my hand, but here there is not the torch."

"We can imagine them," Andy told her.

And they could. Even in her bandana skirt and blouse, she could still make one think of flames that burned low at the start and then grew to racing wildness. Beany saw a side of Ofila she had but glimpsed before—the exotic, bewitching prima donna. She could even understand why Ofila gave herself such airs.

Carlton and Miss Cirisi watched for a while and then went into his office. To juggle that bare-bones budget, Beany thought.

Ofila brought her dance to a swift end. "That is finish. When the torches burn close to hands, then I dive into ocean."

Elena's brother came forward to say, "Our papa said that I should bring Elena home at ten. We have room for four others."

The party broke up. Beany heard all the arguing about which of the Hikers would have room in his car for which of the girls. Happiness was thick in Beany's throat. The Ho Ho party was a success.

Miss Cirisi told Beany. "I knew we needed someone like you to warm things up out here."

Beany and Andy ran through the rain to his car as Carlton called out, "We'll get out early in the morning to the pool, Beany."

"Rain or no rain?"

"Rain or no rain," he repeated with a wry smile.

189

On Barberry Street, Andy drove into the Malone driveway and turned off his motor. The nicest part about a date with Andy was the post-mortem afterwards.

She murmured again, "You saved the party from falling flat on its face, Andy. I was just sick. And then you stepped in—or rather Mexican-Hat-Danced in—"

He chuckled, changed the subject. "Your Ofila is quite a number."

"She's not my number-one problem any more. She couldn't be nicer. Andy, I had a feeling when she was dancing— Did you get the idea that she was showing off for Carlton? I mean, did you notice that when he disappeared into his office, she brought it to a quick *feenish?*"

"Sure, I noticed it. You were dumb not to have caught on before."

"Oh, murder!" Beany breathed.

So that was why Ofila seemed downright pleased to have a skinned elbow so she could wait in Carlton's office, even as Violetta, for him to "banditch" it. That was why Ofila preened herself so over the gift of the lace mantilla.

Beany mused, "I guess I never thought about *her* being so dumb as to make a play for Carlton. Of course, from the time she came up from Mexico, he's been doing all sorts of things to help her—"

"And she's a conceited little *señorita* who misreads them. Probably in Mexico young men don't help young ladies learn a language, or enter them in high-diving and give them the run of the pool. Unless they have intentions. That's why she was gunning for you at first. She figured you were competition."

"Oh, no. She couldn't think that."

But even as she said it, several thoughts pushed into her mind. Miss Joanne, of the sun-bleached blond hair, tossing off, "Your being a friend of Carlton Buell will make it that much harder for you down here." The knowing glances Mrs. Harper and Miss Kunitani exchanged whenever Beany mentioned Ofila's animosity. And Ofila's animosity *had* ended the very afternoon Andy came to Lilac Way with Father Hugh, and the gigglers had asked Beany if he were her beau. So that was it. Hm-mm.

Unconsciously she quoted Miss Joanne, "Carl's just as naïve as the Bobbsey twins about what goes on in Ofila's head. Somebody ought to tell him, Andy."

"Somebody ought to mind her own business. Carl can look out for himself."

Beany laughed comfortably. "Yes, I guess I better feel sorry for Ofila—or any girl that got ideas about Mr. Bull."

Beany talked on about all the happenings at Lilac Way. She came to Dulcie and Trighorn. "He took her repaired bag back to her, and they went dancing at Acacia Gardens and she told me—"

He joined in, in a mimicking voice, "—and she told me she saw Andy Kern out there—"

"Dancing with a luscious redhead. She tossed that off and left it to fester."

Again Andy's hearty laugh. "I saw Dulcie's eyes bug out when she saw me with Sylvia. I wondered how long it would take her to tell you."

"Sylvia who? She's pretty, I suppose, and doesn't have freckles."

"Never mind the who. Yes, she's pretty enough to win a beauty contest that the South Denver merchants put on last year, and I doubt if she'll ever forget it. She was in my class at junior high and then she went out here to Huxley Hall. Darnedest thing, but that gal has always had some allure for me. I've had dates with her now and then for a long time."

"Andy, I didn't know you were nursing a secret passion all these years. All the time I trusted you. That's the way with men." And she sang out loudly. " 'A false-hearted lover is worse than a thief—' "

He thumped her scoldingly on the back. "Hush, you dope. You'll have all your family descending on the man who betrayed you."

They sat in silence while the rain ticked on the top of the car, and then he said, "Remember that day when I drove you downtown to the *Call* and you were telling about all the talks you seniors had listened to about standing at the crossroads of life? I guess it's about that time for all of us. Mary Fred, and her tackling a new job. Even Dulcie and her wondering if she should get out of car-hopping—"

"Don't try to get my mind off Sylvia who doesn't have freckles."

Again that thump on the back. "How I hate an interrupting woman. Try to tell 'em something, and it's chip-chip-chip."

"I won't say another word. We're at the crossroads of life."

"We're at the crossroads of life," he said, and there was a sober note in his voice. "And here's old linthead Andy looking at the road he wants to follow and wondering if he's got what it takes. And thinking that he'd better be sure he isn't leaving any loose ends. And that brings us back to Sylvia and her haunting fascination for me."

"You mean Sylvia's a loose end?"

"No. Not now. The old hang-over from junior high is no more. You ought to understand, Knucks. I remember bumping into that crazy hold Norbett Rhodes had on you when I first knew you."

"And then all at once I was over it. And I felt so—so set free. Now when I see Norbett it's—it's as though the Beany that was so ga-ga over him was another Beany Malone."

"Same here. With Sylvia. After that trial run at Acacia Gardens."

Curiosity nagged at Beany. But she knew Andy would never go into more details about Sylvia. She mused on, "Mary Fred always says that you are a different *you* as you go through life."

"That's right."

A gust of rain drove against the car windows. "Another swimming session in the morning." She shivered. "This time next week the lifesaving test will be over. I'll either be awfully glad—or awfully sad."

"I'm sorry I won't be here to congratulate or console you. I'm getting my two weeks' leave. Started today."

"You won't be here? Where're you going?"

"I don't know. I just want to get away—maybe I'll go to our relatives in Wyoming. Or maybe where there are trees to chop down. Nothing like swinging an ax to help think things over."

Beany's mind went back to last Christmastime when Andy's sister Rosellen died suddenly—complications from a broken rib and the polio she'd had as a child. Rosellen on crutches had still been the bright star to everyone who knew her. At that time, too, Andy in bitter grief had fled his family and Beany to get off by himself and chop down Christmas trees.

She said softly, "I thought of Rosellen all the time the girls and I made skirts and blouses and planned the party because—"

He squeezed her hand in understanding, quoted, " 'She always was the gayest at the party.' "

A long silence, and then Beany asked, "What do you have to think over? Tell me more."

"Not yet, Old Curiosity Shop. After all, I'm still a Marine with a few more months to serve." Again that undertone of soberness that had baffled Beany before. "I'll tell you this, Speckleface. The luckiest day of my life was the day you walked into our French class and I thought, 'Now there's a girl who wears her heart in her eyes. And it's very becoming.' "

"Goodness, Andy, you sound awfully last-will-and-testament."

"Just famous last words. There's a letup in the rain. Come on, let's sprint for it. Or you won't be able to roll out at five in the morning."

195

At the doorway he kissed her on the cheek. "For luck next Saturday on your date with Admiral Blesek."

She wanted to say, "Andy, you're *different*. What is all this talk about *crossroads*? What is it you aren't telling me?"

But Andy was already leaping down the steps and running through the rain to his car.

16

A DRIZZLY rain still fell from dark skies the next morning when Red nudged Beany to wakefulness. She groaned herself off the pillow and onto the shag rug by her bed. It seemed hardly fair to expect a human to get up when the sun stayed in bed.

Ugh! Her swim suit which she plucked from the back of a chair near the window and wriggled into was clammy cold. Instead of her short beach jacket, she bundled herself into her terry-cloth robe, picked up the lifesaving book, and went down the stairs to where Carlton waited.

"That's certainly a soggy expression you're wearing this morning," he greeted her.

"I'm not even sure it's morning. Should we take an umbrella to keep from getting rained on in the pool?"

She could sense a grim urgency in Carlton. As they drove toward Crescent Drive and the Buell pool, he said, "Open the book, Beany, and read me that part—about page 120—on the preliminary requirements for a swimmer to start rescue training."

She read aloud, " 'A swimmer who wishes to undertake swimming rescue training should be able to make a shallow dive in good form—' "

"You need to get more distance in yours."

" '—and swim a quarter of a mile without resting, or keep afloat by treading water and swimming in place for a period of ten minutes—' "

"No hanging onto the rail," Carlton put in.

" 'His category of strokes should contain as a minimum, a good side stroke, one of the hand-over-hand strokes (crawl, trudgen or trudgen-crawl) and a fair semblance of a breast stroke. He should be able to swim with ease on the back, using the legs alone for a distance of twenty yards or more. He should, of course, be capable of making a surface dive and of swimming a short distance underwater.' "

"Admiral Blesek can spot any weakness," Carlton put in.

He had quoted the admiral to Beany until he loomed in her mind as a giant ogre with gimlet eyes.

Their sandaled feet trod over sodden lawn to the high fence around the pool. Carlton unlocked the gate. No caretaker Gallagher was in sight, and Beany thought enviously of his sleeping soundly this dour Sunday morning.

How exacting Carlton was. He drilled her in diving from the side of the pool, both standing and running. "Get distance in it." And the surface dive. "If a *person* were on the bottom, you couldn't take two or three stabs to get down to him."

A halfhearted sun was out when they practiced holds and the breaking of them on the tiled apron of the pool. Gallagher appeared in his Sunday suit, and told Carlton, "Your uncle Matthew is here. He wants you both to come in and have coffee with him."

Uncle Matthew was younger and less pompous than Carlton's father, Beany decided, as she shook hands with him and sank down on a metal chair in the breakfast room off the kitchen. She voiced her appreciation for the use of the pool, and then asked him about his vacationing family.

His unmarried daughter, he told her, had gone to Mexico City for an intensive course in Spanish at the university there. His wife had decided at the last minute to go with her.

"We didn't feel right about a twenty-year-old girl being on her own down there. They'd like me to drive down and get them when the course is over. But I've got a case in court that might drag out too long."

Fortified by coffee and a sweet roll, Carlton was on his feet again with a "Come on, Beany."

Later they were joined in the pool by Uncle Matthew's married daughter Emily and her four-year-old Johnny. He splashed in the shallow water while Emily, in the deep end, entered into the lifesaving drill and lent herself as a willing victim for Beany's approaches and carries.

The sun was high overhead when Carlton walked over to his clothes and wrist watch and said, "O.K., Beany. I can get you home in time for the last Mass at St. Mary's."

From Monday through Friday that following week the sun came up and went down on Beany's perfecting her lifesaving technique. Rear approach and chin carry. Underwater approach and lifting the victim out of the pool. The fireman's carry and resuscitation.

Emily was never there in the morning, but came for an hour or two with her little boy for practice in the evening. She was always praiseful and encouraging. "You're getting better and better," she would tell Beany.

Mr. Bull, all tense anxiety, wasted no time in praise or encouragement.

Friday evening. And the final workout before Beany went to the Y pool the next day to demonstrate her ability to the faultfinding Admiral Blesek. She and Carlton left Lilac Way early and took the familiar route to the Matthew Buell home on Crescent Drive.

"We'll go over the works tonight," Carlton said. "Then tomorrow you take all day off. Sleep late, and just take it easy until you go down to the Y."

"To my doom. I'm scared to death."

"So was I when I took it. Don't panic. I mean, suppose you don't do a good enough surface dive to reach the bottom and bring up the weight. All right. Come to the surface, gulp in some air—let it out, and go down again."

"I suppose Emily will come over again to work with us?"

"Not this evening. I'll be your victim. Drowners aren't always as docile as Emily has been for you. This is going to be practice in handling the grabbers and the clutchers."

Perhaps it was because they were both tense and worried about tomorrow's outcome that the session got off to a bad start. Beany's header into the water was too flat. "I can imagine what Blesek will think of a belly flop

201

like that," Carlton said. While he explained how to break the grip on the wrist, and Beany held to the rail, he snapped, "Don't be a rail-holder. It's just as easy to tread water."

The blocking and breaking of the victim's holds. Beany had gone through it all in a halfhearted way at Harkness High. She had practiced on Emily again and again. But those efforts were a far cry from working with a grim Mr. Bull who, in deep water, clutched her around the neck, or fastened a tight grip on her ankle.

She would flounder about, breathing in both air and water while he said with the thin patience of a kindergarten teacher, "Breathe *out* through your nose, *in* through your mouth. Here, let me show you. Grab me anyplace—around the neck or the wrist or the knees, and see how I block you off."

He did it with expert ease. "If the push in the chest doesn't work," he'd add, "then bring up your foot and give a shove—not a kick—in the stomach. It isn't lifesaving in the strictest sense, but you have to know what to do in an emergency."

The sinking sun was turning the water deep violet, and still Carlton was saying, "Now use the fireman's carry and take me to shallow water."

Beany gritted her teeth, ducked herself under him, rolled him onto her shoulders and carried him, her hundred and fourteen pounds bent under his hundred and sixty. "If you'd had my weight divided evenly, I wouldn't have seemed so heavy," he said.

"Be awfully careful," she panted out, "or you might make a mistake and say an encouraging word."

His voice was chill. "The buttering-up department is closed tonight. It's the night before the test, remember? Do the fireman's carry over."

Tension built up as the sun went down.

More drill on resuscitation. Carlton lay beside the pool while Beany knelt at his head, lifting his arm, pressing down on his back ribs. "No, that's too fast. Time it. Say to yourself, 'Out goes the bad air; in comes the good.' And press harder with your hands—I can barely feel the pressure."

What did he think she was made of? Cast iron?

She was bone-tired and looked longingly toward the little pile of jackets and sandals and towels. But Carlton was scrambling to his feet. "Once more. The panicky-swimmer rescue."

She watched him dive in and reach the middle of the pool in three strokes. Wearily she dived in and swam toward him. He grabbed her around the shoulders, and, following his instructions as well as those in the book, she submerged. (The victim will let go to come up for air, the book said.) But the rescuer, coming up for air,

203

found the victim some distance away waiting to try some other ruthless trick on her.

In frustrated anger she turned her back to him, swam to the edge of the pool and climbed out. She had just picked up her towel when he was beside her. He took it out of her hands as though she were a stubborn child. "We're not finished yet."

"I am. I've had it. I'm going home."

"Not yet you aren't."

Her voice was shrill and shaky. "Look, I'm not one of your Bombshells that you can bully." She mimicked, " 'One more deal like that, and we'll be getting a new pitcher.' You're not Mr. Bull to me. You're just Carl that I taught to rumba. And I'm not your cowed little Angelo. I'm Beany Malone, remember?"

"Sure, you're Beany Malone. Tell that to the admiral tomorrow. Tell him that, after all, you're one of the specially privileged, so you'd like a special lifesaving test, and one of their nice bargain emblems to wear on your suit."

"It was your idea—this whole crazy idea of my being a lifesaver. It was your idea for me to go down to Lilac Way in the first place. You can't say I encouraged you."

Another person would have shouted back in anger. Not Carlton Buell. He didn't raise his voice to say, "Just turn off the tantrum, Beany. And get this straight.

You've got to know how to rescue a panicky swimmer. And you're not leaving this pool till you do."

With a watery eye she measured his dripping, determined figure. Furious as she was, she didn't pick up the towel.

He walked away from her and said at the edge of the pool, "Use the cross-chest carry and then lift me out of the pool."

He dived in. So did she. Anger and a stubborn, "I'll show him," gave her strength. She approached him, and he fastened his grip on her shoulder again. O.K., he'd told her what to do. She brought up her foot and gave him not a firm push in the chest, but a vicious kick that caught him in both the chest and chin.

His hold broken, she whirled him about and pulled him toward her for the cross-chest carry. She swam with him to the edge, taking malicious satisfaction in *not* keeping his head out of the water all the time.

If he could play it tough, so could she. She clamped first one of his hands on the tiled edge and then the other. She hoisted out the top of his body, then his legs, not caring whether they bruised against the edge of the pool or not.

She left him in his prone position, stalked over and picked up her towel and mopped at her dripping face.

Carlton did the same. Without a word, they slid wet feet into sandals and pulled on limp jackets that stuck to their wet bodies. Without a word they drove homeward. Again as they drove down College Boulevard, the flashing neon sign told them that shrimps-in-a-boat were being served at the Ragged Robin. But Carlton's glance never lifted from the road ahead.

He stopped in front of the Malone house and left the motor running. She could see that his set chin was reddened by her kick that should have been only a shove in the chest. His very dignified silence increased her guilt—and her anger.

She ground out, "I know what's eating you. You're ashamed for your Admiral Blesek to know you coached me. Well, you needn't worry. I won't tell him." Even as she said it, a small inner voice reminded her, "Look at all the time and work Carlton's given to it."

"You don't have to tell him. I've already told him. I told him when I phoned to find out about the test."

"Oh! So you're afraid I'll disgrace you. All right, then I won't go down at all and make a fool of myself—and you."

Oh, no, this was not good old Carl next door. This was a stony-faced young man who said evenly, "If that's the way you want it, all right. Just call Miss Cirisi in the morning and tell her so she can find someone else for Lilac Way."

He was out of the car and opening the door for her, and walking with her through the gate. Always the gentleman, Beany thought. He'd walk a girl to the door even if she did kick him in the chin.

17

LATE as it was, Beany was not the latest of the
Malones to return to dinner. But, for that matter, there
was no dinner to return to.

Mary Fred came in a few steps behind her. She had
been out to the Carmody farm riding and, not quite
trustful of old Charlie, had stayed on to feed and curry
her mare.

Adair had been detained at an art exhibit. She was
sitting in the hall at the telephone, talking to Martie
Malone who was in Chicago. She came out in the
kitchen to say, "He hopes he'll be back tomorrow." She
picked up a can of biscuits she had evidently put down
when the phone rang, and asked Beany, "It doesn't take
very long for these to bake, does it?"

"Not after the oven is hot," Beany said wearily, and turned her attention to Johnny who had opened a can of tuna fish and was slivering onion in it. "What do you expect to come out with there?" she asked.

"It could be tuna salad," he told her, "if you slice a few hard-boiled eggs on top. For me, it's going between a couple chunks of bread to eat on my way to the TV station."

He took a sample bite, and then bolted out the door.

Beany leaned on in the doorway and said fretfully, "I'm so hungry my knees are hollow. I just wish there was a decent meal to come home to like other people have."

She knew she was being unreasonable. But she was dog-tired, and scared—and heartsick over her quarrel with Carlton. . . . Surely he knew she didn't mean what she said about not going down to take the lifesaving test tomorrow. It was all she could do to keep from crying.

Adair said, "Oh, Beany, it *is* a shame—these catch-as-catch-can meals. Now that we're all so busy, I wish we could find someone who would come in and cook a good dinner for us."

The thought of Elena Zakowski flitted through Beany's mind. Elena had not been working since the fracas with Mrs. Morrison over the bracelet. Beany had meant to talk to her about a part-time job at the

Malones'. But that was just one other thing that had been crowded out by the distance dive and the underwater approach.

Mary Fred was making her usual clatter—lighting the oven and finding a pan for the biscuits. As usual, her jodhpur boots were in the middle of the floor. But she stopped her banging to say, "Little Beaver, you look drowned and done in. Get out of that wet suit. No man in the dorm, so skin it off there in the hall, and I'll run up and get your robe."

"I'll make you some hot tea," Adair said.

The three womenfolks were still sitting at the dining table in tired lassitude, when the front door opened and closed with a bang, and a familiar voice called out, "Anybody home?"

Beany directed her, "In the dining room, Dulcie."

Dulcie came through the living room and stopped in the doorway. Again she was in carhop uniform of short flared skirt and drum majorette boots. But tonight her feet fairly danced in the boots, and her pony tail had a perky bounce.

"I have something to show you. If you have dark glasses at hand, put them on so you won't be blinded." And with her usual love of drama, she held up her left hand. All eyes rested on the fourth finger and the diamond ring that flashed under the crystal chandelier.

She beamed in happy delight at their surprised faces.

"From Norbett?" Beany exclaimed.

"Norbett! You *are* behind the times. From Trig."

"Trig? Trig who?" Mary Fred asked.

"Trighorn. His first name is August. Augie, his mother calls him, but I like *Trig*. It's right for him. Oh, I know what you're thinking—that it's fast work. O.K., but when you see a good thing, grab it, I always say. And he wasn't so slow in asking me either. He couldn't wait to put this ring on. This is the slack time at the Robin before the after-show rush—also feed-the-ulcer time for the boss—so I had to run down and tell you and show you, because—well, Trig is so wonderful and I'm so—"

"You're going to be married?" Beany asked when Dulcie paused for a breath.

"This fall. Summer is his busiest time—you know, he practically runs that bottling works. But he'll get two weeks in September. Adair, I thought a lot about your talking to me about pulling myself up by my own bootstraps so the bright boys wouldn't look down on me. Yeah, and about going on to college and art school and studying design and textiles. I even thought about your putting pasteboard in your shoes so you could stay on and study in all those places in Europe—"

Adair laughed. "My pasteboard days were only in Rome."

"And I thought about that snooty Norbett and how I was so left out of all his friends' talk about some Russian writer that influenced so many other writers—"

"Dostoevsky?" Mary Fred queried.

"Maybe. I can't pronounce it much less spell it. Anyway, he influenced one of our boys that won the Nobel award—"

"Faulkner," Mary Fred filled in again.

"So he influenced Faulkner. I couldn't see myself getting in a sweat about it like all of them that sat around that night—those girls in their drab sweaters, and one didn't even wear lipstick. It's just like Adair says, you have to want something awfully hard to dedicate your life to it. I'm not the brainy or self-sacrificing type. And then I met Trig and felt right at home with him, and right at home with his folks. His mother's just swell—and he's got a sister that I showed how to make a dress like my new polka dot. Anyway, I even thought about all that at-the-crossroads stuff they hand out at school. You know,

'Not what we see, but what we choose— ' "

212

Adair, with her memory for quotations, finished,

> " *'These are the things that mar or bless*
> *The sum of human happiness.'* "

Dulcie twisted the diamond ring on her finger, and said with disarming candor, "I never felt at home with the campus kids that took me out. Even if one of them had fallen for me, and I'd fallen in love with him—it still wouldn't have been right. Take Norbett and all his big talk. Can you imagine his aunt—that social-climbing old ewe!—ever buddying up to me? It isn't only that Trig and I are in love—it's that he fits into my family, and I fit into his. One reason I used to come here and dress, and have my dates pick me up here—well, Beany, you know what our house is like."

Beany's heart went out to her. The Lungaarde dwelling was out beyond the university in a district where new cheap houses vied along dirt roads with old, run-down ones.

Not only that, but Dulcie's carpenter father was building an addition on to their house in his spare time. One had to skirt around cinder blocks, piles of used lumber, and old shabby trucks full of sand to get to the front door.

"But Trig—why, the very first night he came and brought my purse, he and Dad worked together to take our old sink out." She lifted luminous eyes to Adair and said defensively, "I don't want a future bad enough to wear old worn-out shoes. I like new, pretty ones too well. I don't want to be a dress designer. I just want to make clothes Trig thinks I'm pretty in—and hunt for remnants for slip covers for our house. I guess you'll think I'm all wrong not to have higher goals."

"Indeed, I don't. No sir," Adair assured her. "I think you're right, honey. You've thought it through and you know what you want—"

"I want a man and a house and kids," Dulcie said.

"Don't we all!" Mary Fred put in fervently.

Dulcie drew from her pocket samples of white brocade and lace, and babbled happily on, "I'm going to make my own wedding dress. I looked at one that cost eighty-nine-fifty, and I can make it for about twenty-three. . . ."

"Won't you be going back to Harkness next year?" Beany asked. Dulcie had been a semester behind Beany.

"Nah. I couldn't graduate next year anyway, what with failing chem and math. I don't care. Trig quit when he was a soph. Beany, we want you for our bridesmaid. Trig thinks you're the swellest person he ever knew."

"That's right," Mary Fred said. "Beany played Cupid in bringing you two together."

"It was more than that," Dulcie said. "Some girl down at Lilac Way made him feel like an illiterate lout, and then Beany came along— He'll be your friend for life, Beany."

"He's swell," Beany said warmly. She stirred with an uncomfortable thought. Was she snobbish to be thinking: But I wouldn't want to marry a man that quit school when he was fifteen?

Dulcie glanced at her watch and leaped to her feet. "Again I must race the boss back to the Robin. I'd hate to get fired before I pay for my wedding dress."

Even then she lingered in the doorway to add, "There isn't anything Trig can't do. I happened to mention once that I liked these wall ovens, and he said he could cut one in our kitchen wall."

A lusty bang of the door, and Dulcie, with diamond, was gone.

Adair murmured, "Yes, it's so right for her. Can't you just see her in the years ahead, stitching up layettes, and cooking Sunday dinner for his folks? That's their world—and they'll be happy."

At bedtime, Beany sat in front of her dressing table, taking a snip here and there in her short hair with the

215

manicure scissors. No wisp of hair must becloud her vision for her crucial test in the Y pool tomorrow. . . . Yes, surely Carlton knew she had spoken out of temper and tiredness. Once she glanced out the window toward the Buell residence, wondering about telephoning him and saying, "Carl, I didn't mean it."

But the Buell house was dark.

Mary Fred came in, in her pajamas and dropped down on Beany's bed to comb her hair. "I certainly felt like an old spinster aunt when Dulcie flashed her diamond and showed samples of her wedding dress."

Beany nodded. "Me, too—that always-a-bridesmaid-but-never-a-bride feeling."

Mary Fred brushed her brown, curly hair and thought aloud, "As Adair said, it's so right for Dulcie to marry Trighorn. But I couldn't help thinking it wouldn't be so right for one of Martie Malone's kids, would it?"

"I thought that, too."

Mary Fred went on thinking aloud, "I wouldn't like the feeling that other people were talking over my head—or my husband's. Not that I'm one of these cultural snobs. I'd even like a guy who could put in a wall oven—but I'd want him to know who Faulkner was."

Beany put down her scissors thoughtfully. It was even hard to think things through with tomorrow's test heavy on her spirits. She got up and, going to her closet, took out a full cotton skirt and worked the zipper back and forth. "Do you suppose a zipper will work all right underwater?"

"Pens do," Mary Fred said. "Though I've never tried."

"I'll wear this skirt and a short-sleeved, button-down-the-front blouse over my swim suit. One of the first things we do in our test tomorrow is to undress in the water."

"Hm-mm. That'd be no time for a gal to wear a girdle."

18

THERE were five who were taking the lifesaving test.

In the entrance of the Y, Beany picked them out by their tense look and the waterproof bags which held swim suits and the extra clothing for that worrisome feat of disrobing in the water. They even gravitated together with nervous greetings while they waited for Admiral Blesek.

Three were college-age boys. Two had come together and had the same slim, wiry build. They wore identical Levis, T-shirts, and crewcuts. They both chewed gum with deadly earnestness. The other was the athletic hero type. "Colo. U." was lettered on one side of his canvas bag, and "J. Burton" on the other.

A middle-aged and solidly built woman was taking the test, too. She wore a flowered print dress and flowered hat; her plastic bag had a floral pattern in it.

She did most of the talking while they waited for the admiral, and the two boys chewed their gum, and J. Burton stood next to Beany, who wondered how he could keep his long, wavy hair back in the water. The woman's name she told them was Dora Warfel, and she and her sister ran a vacation camp in the mountains— "Maybe you've heard of Kinnikinnick Camp?"

The wavy-haired boy was carrying on his own conversation with Beany. He had come down from Boulder for the test and was going to stay over and hear Belafonte at the D.U. stadium, and had Beany ever heard him?

"Just on recordings—" She broke off to murmur, "That must be Admiral Blesek." For the man coming through the door and toward them carried a waterproof bag as well as a brief case.

He was neither a giant nor an ogre, but a roly-poly tanned Santa Claus in summer attire. A brisk shaking of hands all around while he said, "We'll take the written exam upstairs first."

The Kinnikinnick woman stood or walked beside him as they took the elevator and went down a hall to a room with a long table and chairs around it. She talked on

219

about the new pool at their camp, while the wavy-haired boy told Beany that he was on the swimming team at Colorado U., and the two crewcuts walked silently together.

Oh, dear, Beany wished Pretty Boy wouldn't stick so close. He was even holding out a chair for her. She was relieved when the admiral said as he handed each one a long sheet of mimeographed questions, "Scatter yourselves out around the table. You're all adults, so I won't need to stress no talking."

Beany's ballpoint wobbled in her fingers as she answered the first question. Carlton had told her the written test would not be hard. It wasn't. Not after her near memorizing of all that was in the Red Cross book.

The admiral who, in glasses, looked like a pudgy school teacher, began reading the answers as each one finished and handed his paper to him. The woman in her flowery hat was the last to complete hers. The five sat waiting anxiously while he ran his eyes over the pages.

Evidently all were satisfactory, for he shuffled them together, reached for his brief case. "So far so good. We'll go to the pool now. They've cleared it for us till the six o'clock class. That should give us time. Put on your clothes as quickly as you can over your swim suits." His eyes twinkled. "The clothes you'll be taking off right away."

The talky woman said brightly, "When you run a camp, you get to be a quick-change artist."

Down the hall again, down the elevator with the same pairing off, the woman now telling Admiral Blesek about a new method she had devised for teaching children to swim.

Beany's new admirer told her the *J* stood for Jerry, and resumed his talk about Belafonte— "In case you're wondering, I'm leading up to ask you to go with me," he said with a bright smile that another time Beany might have found appealing.

But how could she give thought to Belafonte or a very buddy-o boy named Jerry with this crisis ahead?

In the hallway from which doors led to the ladies' and men's dressing rooms, the admiral halted. "I want to say this to all of you. This is not an easy or pleasant task for me. I know that in most of your cases, a job hangs on your passing this test. I hate to fail you. But remember, if you do fail this time, you can work on your weakness and take it again."

Did his eyes linger dubiously on Beany Malone?

"I've given this test to friends—to sons and daughters of friends. But the minute we reach the pool all friendship ceases. My own son could be taking the test, and I'd still ask myself the same question: If my wife, my children were drowning, would I trust him to save them?"

As they turned away, Jerry Burton muttered to Beany, "Our coach gave us that same pitch when he picked the swim team."

Beany was soon ready. White blouse, full skirt over her sun-and-water-bleached turquoise suit. She memorized again: One button on skirt band, zipper. She had even, at Johnny's suggestion, rubbed soap on the zipper so it wouldn't stick. Three buttons on blouse. She had practiced at home till the buttons slid out easily. Keds and socks.

If only the woman wouldn't talk, talk, talk over the dressing-room partition all the while she changed. She asked Beany to fasten the back straps of her swim suit. It, too, had flowers in it. And on the green cap she pulled on was a scattering of plastic daisies. "I notice the children at our camp like me to look pretty," she said as she fastened skirt and blouse.

"Ready?" Beany asked, moving toward the door.

The woman patted Beany's tense back. "You're nervous, aren't you, dearie? That's no way to approach even a minor crisis in your life. We only make it harder on ourselves by not having confidence."

The wiry crewcuts had discarded their gum. Hm-mm —and Jerry was keeping his hair back with a wide, white elastic band.

The admiral had looked roly-poly in his gray suit. In his maroon trunks with the lifesaving emblem on the left side, he showed up chunky, and hard-muscled as a blacksmith.

The undressing in the water came first. Five dives into deep water. Five swimmers bobbing and ducking about. "Throw your shoes and socks on the edge of the pool," Admiral Blesek shouted. Beany's first shoe landed neatly; the second missed. A black head with a white band billowed close to her, and Jerry said, "Never mind. I'll get it for you later."

Her skirt next. Zippers did work underwater. She tied the skirt into a safety float which ballooned beside her while she wriggled out of her blouse. She glanced about. The boys had finished. Their three pairs of Levis were like large, blue sausages floating on the water.

Mrs. Kinnikinnick was the last to finish.

The surface dive to bring up a ten-pound weight next. Each boy dived with ease—pointed toes the last thing visible before the swimmer appeared clutching the long piece of iron. Again the college boy muttered a helpful hint to Beany, "It's got a hole in the center. Crook your finger into it so it won't slide out of your hands."

Beany had to make two tries for it. Hole in the middle or no, it still slid out of her grip. She came to the surface, took her "bite" of air, snorted it out, and went down again.

Admiral Blesek nodded as she held it above water, motioned her to drop it for the last tryer, the woman from Kinnikinnick Camp. She tried ineffectually several times until the admiral called to her, "Let it go now. We'll come back to it. We'll get on with the carries."

The test went on with scarcely a hitch. The front approach, the rear, and underwater. The tired swimmer, the head carry.

They worked in pairs, with the admiral diving in now and then and acting as victim to make it come out even. I hope I don't draw him, Beany worried; he weighs *over* two hundred. She was grateful when she drew the woman to demonstrate the cross-chest, and one of the crewcuts for the fireman's carry.

Admiral Blesek blew his whistle.

"Now we come to the real test of the lifesaver—the rescue of the panicky swimmer who fights against his rescuer because he has lost all reason. I want you victims to make it hard for your rescuer. The rescuer will bring in his victim, lift him out of the pool, and practice artificial respiration on him. This is the whole treatment."

Beany, treading water in the deep part of the pool, watched with wholesome respect as her Belafonte fan rescued one of the crewcuts. The victim grabbed his arm, and the rescuer broke that hold; the victim grabbed him about the neck, and both went underwater. The rescuer somehow twisted him about and fastened him to his chest with a tight arm. Beany watched the dark head with the white band wend a sure way to the pool's edge with his burden.

All three of the boys were experts, she realized. There was no doubt but that by the time they dived into a pool again, the W.S.I. emblem would be sewed on their trunks.

Beany acted as "clutcher and grabber" for the same crewcut when he had been resuscitated.

Admiral Blesek looked up from the chart he was marking to the woman who was holding onto the rail. (She hadn't been drilled by Mr. Bull.) "Warfel, you're the rescuer." He indicated the other crewcut, "You're the hard–to–rescue swimmer."

Beany watched as the woman swam out to the boy in the middle of the pool. He, acting his part, floundered in the water and at her approach grabbed her forearm with both hands. The daisy cap went under. The would-be victim came to the surface first, watching for his would-be rescuer to appear.

225

She did—threshing and flailing wildly. The roles were suddenly reversed. Her frantic hands clawed at the boy in panic that was not simulated. Beany saw the jolted look on his face as he backed away from her, not knowing what to do.

Then, as her hands kept clutching at his short bristly hair, as Admiral Blesek stepped in alarm to the edge of the pool, the boy grasped the situation. Swiftly he caught one of the woman's wrists, pulled her under his arm and onto his chest, and struck out with her.

It was all so unbelievable—so jolting.

The boy would have used the out-of-the-pool lift on her, but when he placed her hand on the edge and started to climb out, she suddenly wrenched away from him with a strangled cry of, "I'm all right—I'm all right!" and reached for the ladder. But he steadied her on it, and Admiral Blesek leaned over to take her hand as she stepped onto the wet tile. She kept repeating in shrill hysteria, "I'm all right, I tell you. I'm all right."

She looked about with dazed eyes—at the swimmers, at the heavy-set man beside her. And then, without a word and with her daisy cap askew and a pitiful attempt at dignity, she turned and faltered her way up the two steps to the door of the ladies' dressing room.

Beany felt aching fellow sympathy. . . . The woman had called her dearie, and told her to have confidence.

She climbed out of the pool and asked Admiral Blesek, "Should I go in with her?"

He eyed her a thoughtful moment before he shook his head. "I don't think so. I think maybe she'd rather be alone."

An awkward silence fell. Beany backed up against the tiled wall for support. The dark-haired Jerry backed up alongside her. If he makes one snide crack about that poor woman, I'll hate him, she thought. He didn't say a word but took the elastic band off his head, smoothed it carefully, and put it on again.

The crewcut who had started out to be the victim and ended up being the rescuer, muttered uncomfortably, "Gosh, I didn't know what to do—"

"You did the only thing you could do," the admiral said.

Beany could only think: The boys don't have to worry. But I still have to rescue a fighting swimmer. She folded her arms over the cold shakiness in her middle.

Admiral Blesek walked to the low edge of the diving board and picked up his pencil and pad. In the silence they could hear the din and noise in the men's dressing room. Two young boys pushed through the door, and the admiral motioned them back. "We'll be out shortly, fellows."

He came back to the waiting four. "Let's see now. Who hasn't pulled in a panicky swimmer?"

"I haven't," Beany said in a thin voice.

Jerry Burton said, "I guess it's my turn to be her victim."

Admiral Blesek's keen eyes raked over him, rested on Beany. She could almost read his mind. He had probably noticed the boy's friendly overtures to her, and he was thinking, I won't use him, because he'll make it easy for her.

And that's fine with me, Beany thought hopefully. I'd rather bring in one of the crewcuts because either one is smaller than Jerry.

The admiral said crisply, "I'll be your victim, Malone."

Beany's heart plummeted to her wet heels. Maybe he had felt all along that she wasn't good enough, and he was taking this way to show her up.

"All right?" But the way he said it, it wasn't a question. "Bring me across the pool, out, and resuscitation."

She watched him dive in, desperately conscious of his thick arms, his tree trunks of legs.

And then in the brief minute it took him to get across the pool, she thought of Carlton. He had wanted to spare her just such ignominy of failure as she had now

228

witnessed with the woman from Kinnikinnick Camp. All night, all day, that quarrel had weighed on her. This was her chance. If she could just go to him and say, "I pulled out Admiral Blesek," it would make up for her meanness of last night.

She dived in and swam toward her victim, her jaw clamped tight.

Yes, he was giving her the works. When she was but a stroke from him, he dipped out of sight. O.K., Admiral, she thought grimly, I'll fight to the finish. She surface-dived and saw him lying on the bottom of the pool, looking to Beany like nothing but a two-ton blimp. "Throw your feet up and stroke down," Carlton had drilled her.

She reached bottom and the admiral. She took a firm grip on the white canvas belt of his trunks. With her own feet on the pool's bottom, she pushed herself upward. It surprised her that his body lifted to the surface so easily.

She sensed that, once he had caught a breath, he would turn and grab her. She was ready with a block that shoved him away. She reached for his thick wrist and turned him so that his back was toward her.

The cross-chest carry. Stretch as she would, her arm wasn't long enough to reach all the way across that barrel chest. She heard his chuckle. "It *is* quite a circumference."

229

And then came the biggest surprise of the day as with his weight on top of her, she stroked with her left hand and scissored with her feet. He wasn't heavy at all! It was like towing a great balloon. At the pool's edge when she bent over to pull him ashore, he lifted out far more easily than Emily who was only half his weight.

She placed him in position, knelt at his head and pressed down on his back ribs, lifted his arms in rhythm until he said, "That should do it," and scrambled to his feet.

Beany said wonderingly, "I thought you'd be heavier."

His eyes twinkled. "I know. I'm like a porpoise in water. Most fat people are."

He took a moment to pick up his towel and swab it over his face and hair. He said to the four contestants, "This about wraps it up. I'm proud of all of you. I guess you'd like your emblems without delay, eh? I'll give them to you in the lobby as soon as we're dressed."

Beany lingered to say, "I feel bad about the woman— Miss or Mrs. Warfel. If she's in the dressing room, shall I—? I mean, she could have another chance, couldn't she?"

"Sure. Sure. But right now she's a long way from what it takes."

The dressing room was empty. Only a petal from a plastic daisy told that the woman from Kinnikinnick Camp had dressed and left.

Beany got into her clothes so quickly that she was in the lobby even before the admiral and the boys. Admiral Blesek came out first. He handed her the emblem. "You're Carl Buell's pupil, aren't you?"

"Yes, sir." The emblem tight in her hand, she admitted, "I was scared I wouldn't make it."

"I know you were. To tell the truth, I wasn't sure you were enough at home in the water. But when you swam toward me with your jaw squared away, I knew that if I really was in a pickle, you'd pull me in somehow."

Beany hurried down the Y steps. She had no time to waste on chitchat with Jerry Burton. She had but one desire. To show her emblem to Carlton.

She stood in the jostling Saturday evening bustle and pressed the palm of her hand against her ringing ear. A few trickles of water from her wet hair ran down her neck—but that didn't matter. She remembered that she had left one shoe in the bottom of the pool—or had Jerry rescued it as he had promised? That didn't matter either.

A bank clock said six-fifteen. At Lilac Way, the Bombshells would be returning—and Carlton would be with them.

231

A taxi stopped in front of the Y to let out a passenger, and Beany ran toward it. "Do you know where the Lilac Way community center is?" she asked the driver. "Out by the stockyards on Thirty-fourth?" She held out all the money she had—a dollar bill and some silver. "Will this be enough to get me there?"

"I think so, Miss."

She was ashamed of the way she prattled on to the cabdriver about the test, and her hurry to show her emblem—and how if she had taken the bus she would be *forever* getting there. . . . He grinned back at her in the mirror.

He stopped, not in front but at the side of Lilac Way. He took all her money but a dime. "I'll be bighearted and leave you enough for a Coke."

Yes, the Bombshells were back. There was Magee's jeep. She hurried to the outside door of Carlton's office. She couldn't even take time to go through the recreation room and tell Mrs. Harper. Carlton had to be the first to know.

Through the screen door she saw him surrounded by Bombshells, while he rubbed liniment on and wrapped the shoulder of a player who must have been hit by a ball. She waited until they left and stepped in.

She said, "Carl, look!" and held out her Red Cross emblem.

232

He stared at it, at her flushed face—And then with a whoop of exultation he scooped her into his arms. "You made it! Beany, you made it!" And he kissed her.

They held to each other in a glad hysteria, each one tumbling out words. "I couldn't think of anything else all day," he kept saying, while she choked out, "I brought in Admiral Blesek—and he wasn't heavy—"

"*You* brought in Admiral Blesek!"

They were both laughing shakily and talking on. He had been about to drive down to the Y. She had spent all her money for a taxi—except a dime—because she couldn't wait to show him. . . . Her voice was muffled against his shirt that smelled of liniment, against his hard ribs and his heart thumping under them. Inside his arms was haven—the test over—the world shut out. . . .

But the world pushed in, and their arms dropped swiftly.

There was Violetta saying through the screen, "Vince said it was you, Miss Beany, that came in a taxi—and Eugene still sits with a flower for you." And Ofila was saying from the other doorway, "Meestaire Buell, I would like please the aid-band for my elbow."

Carlton didn't answer her but stepped to the doorway to call Mrs. Harper and show her the cloth emblem; to say to one of the children, "Go tell Coach Magee to come in."

Ofila said resentfully, "I have wait, Meestaire Buell, for the aid-band. This afternoon there is bleed from the elbow."

Carlton gave it only brief attention. "Let's try leaving it open, Ofila. Just put on some of the salve." And he dismissed her.

Beany dropped down on the shabby sofa, suddenly limp and trembly. She smiled at Mrs. Harper and Coach Magee and their congratulations. She told them, too, about Admiral Blesek's surprising buoyancy; she talked swimming classes with Magee. But each thump of her heart was reminding her, "Carlton kissed me. He held me tight. . ."

The phone rang, and Carlton handed it to Beany. "It's Johnny. I told him you passed."

Johnny said almost reprovingly, "Beaver! All this worry, all my chewing my nails off up to the elbow for nothing. Pappy's home, and we're living high tonight to celebrate having a lifesaver in the family. Hey, ask Carlton if he can bring you home and eat with us. Otherwise, Dad and I will come after you."

Beany felt a new and strange shyness in turning to Carlton to ask, "Can you take me home? I mean—well, Johnny wants you to help us celebrate."

Lordee, he'd like to, he said, but the Men's Club was meeting at Lilac Way that night to talk over painting the gym.

Martie Malone and Johnny came into Lilac Way and met the staff and talked to them about all the projects that were going on.

As they drove homeward, Beany's father said, "Now that your test is over, Beany, you can put your whole mind and heart on writing those columns for the *Call*. You're right there in what we call the catbird seat."

"Once you get going," Johnny predicted, "the words will pour out faster'n you can keep up with them."

Beany, pinning on the poor wilted flower Eugene had held all day, nodded in agreement. "Yes, I'll get right at it."

But right now her whole mind and heart was taken over by that foolish refrain, "Carlton kissed me. He held me tight."

19

THERE was no understanding Ofila.

For the past weeks she had been amiable and friendly. But that first Monday morning when Beany took over the pool, Ofila's enmity reached from the diving end to the shallow water where Beany taught swimming to small boys and girls. Violetta, Vince, and Freddy were in the class.

"Now pretend you're a duck—a real hungry duck— and dip your head underwater. Open your eyes and look all around. Freddy, don't squint your eyes shut. The water won't hurt them."

Ofila, having won the city meet, was now practicing for the state high-diving finals on Labor Day. Beany had to raise her voice above the thump of the diving board. Ripples from Ofila's wide dives washed over some of the more timid "ducks." And always the recurring clink of silver bracelets touching hoop earrings as she came to the surface and pushed her sodden black mane back from her face.

Yet silence from the deep end was even more disconcerting. Beany would be saying, "Whoof the water out of your nose—see, like a whale—" and look up to see Ofila watching, listening, and sneering.

Sometimes, hearing a titter, Beany would glance up to see Ofila mimicking her for the benefit of the onlookers pressed against the high mesh fence. Exaggerated blowing out through her nose, and a wide, wide opening of her mouth.

Beany would go on with the lesson, self-conscious and irate.

And the one whose ire was even greater was Violetta. "Miss Beany, I could get out and give her a push in the water when her mouth is open so big."

"Never mind, Violetta."

"You should tell Mr. Bull how she makes faces."

"Never mind. Now, children, let's see how many of you can lie flat on the water like logs."

. . . No, this was something she couldn't go running to Mr. Bull with. She *might* mention it if she were still riding to Lilac Way with him in the mornings. But the Men's Club at their meeting Saturday night had voted to paint the walls of the gym. There were volunteers for an early morning shift and for an after-work one. Which meant that Mr. Bull left home long before Beany, and came back late in the evenings.

Beany knew, because her eyes had formed the habit of looking for the light in his room.

And how she scolded herself each time she did it. *What's got into you that you're suddenly mooning over a fellow you've known all your life? So he threw his arms around you and kissed you? You were his pupil, and he was carried away because you passed. So he said he hadn't thought of anything else all day? Sure, because if you'd failed, he'd have been up a stump for someone to drill the kids into being ducks and whales.*

And just don't forget, Miss Beany, that when he had a chance to drive you home ten minutes afterwards, he said he was too busy. Remember?—that's what he told Miss Joanne when she asked him to go to some celebration with her.

At Lilac Way, too, when she caught herself hunting for an excuse to go to his office, the deriding went on. *Don't be an Ofila with the equivalent of a skinned elbow.*

Ofila also carried her cold war to the Ho Ho meetings.

The cooking classes these days were kept busy making sandwiches or nut bread which they left, along with a full coffee maker, as refreshment for the volunteer crew of painters in the gym each evening. It would have been fun if it hadn't been for Ofila's belittling eyes watching Beany's every move.

On Wednesday evening Beany watched the sure movements of Elena Zakowski as she measured water and coffee into the big urn, and she remembered Johnny's saying that morning, "What about this efficient Elena of yours? Could you maybe talk her into coming out and cooking something for the starving Malones?"

Beany detained her to ask, "Elena, you aren't working now, are you? No. What would you think of going to our house and getting dinner for us? You could go out right after the Ho Ho meetings. We'd pay you more than Mrs. Morrison did."

Elena smiled happily. "I'd like it, Miss Beany. But you will have to talk to Papa about it."

Beany walked home with her. Papa Zakowski was working in the yard in his shirt sleeves. When Elena said, "Papa, Miss Beany came home to talk to you," he rolled down his sleeves, buttoned his collar, picked up his coat which lay on the porch, and put it on before he came forward to bow stiffly and shake her hand.

Beany hurried to explain their need of someone to get dinner at their house since she and Mary Fred had jobs—

"And your mother?" he asked. "Does she not cook?"

"She's very busy, too—painting." She decided not to tell him that Adair could paint a family portrait easier than she could get a family meal.

"I'd like to go," Elena said eagerly.

He ignored that remark, and said with grave dignity to Beany, "This is something I must talk about to your father. If he is home tomorrow evening, Mama and I will bring Elena over and call on him. It is better that way. At seven o'clock tomorrow evening we will call."

At seven o'clock that next evening, Beany ushered Papa and Mama Zakowski and Elena into the Malone living room and introduced the four Malones, who had joked beforehand about making a good impression on Papa Z., but who were, nevertheless, stiff and uneasy.

Clearly, this was something one man-of-the-house settled with the other. Neither Mama Zakowski nor Elena said a word. And when Mary Fred said brightly, "We're not hard to please. All we want for dinner is something hot and filling—" the head of the Zakowski household checked her with, "I came to talk to Mr. Malone."

Mr. Malone was so nervous that he filled his pipe and then, without even striking a match to it, tapped the tobacco out. "Well," he stammered, "maybe you'd like to see the kitchen." And to Elena, "We'll show you where

240

we keep the Sinking Fund—that's the money for the groceries."

They all trooped into the kitchen, and Martie Malone took down the oatmeal box. "You see, Elena, you put the household money in here, and reach in it as you need it. If you should run short, just let me know."

Beany contributed, "Sometimes, in an emergency, someone has to borrow—but he has to put in an I.O.U."

Silence, while they all waited for Papa Z.'s decision. He said gravely, "You are good people, and I give permission for Elena to work for you. She will come over by bus after her club meets. While the dinner cooks, she will clean the house." A slight bow to Adair and, "Mrs. Malone, you will see that she does it well."

Beany and Mary Fred exchanged winks as Adair said, "Oh, yes, yes, I will." They couldn't imagine Adair finding fault with the way beds were made or stairs swept.

"At eight o'clock," went on Mr. Zakowski, "one of her brothers will come after Elena."

"If I'm here, I can run her home," Johnny volunteered.

"One of her brothers will come for her," Elena's father repeated. And to his daughter, "Elena, you must take no money out of this Sinking Fund without writing down what it is for. And each evening before you leave, you must take the round box to Mr. Malone to count and see how his money was spent."

Martie Malone gave a start. "But many evenings I won't be here. I'm out of town a great deal, or Adair—Mrs. Malone—and I go out to dinner. We're a fluctuating household, Mr. Zakowski."

He considered that. "Then Elena will have Mr. Johnny count to see that the household money is in order."

Johnny looked equally startled. "But lots of evenings I'm down at the TV station," he said.

"Then it shall wait for Mr. Malone the next evening."

No mention of the womenfolks in all this!

Mary Fred started to say something, but her father silenced her with a shake of his head. He asked shortly of Elena's father, "What is all this to-do about the money? We're not worried about it."

"You do not understand. Elena must be watched. The woman she worked for before was careless. And so Elena stole from her."

Beany saw her father glance at Elena's downcast face. The tightening of his lips meant, as the young Malones had learned, that he had had all that he intended to take.

"I wouldn't call it stealing," he said bluntly. "Elena took the woman's bracelet to show off to the girls. It was a foolish mistake, and I'm sure she regrets it. Elena comes here with our trust, and there'll be no counting of dimes and nickels every night."

Elena lifted grateful cornflower-blue eyes.

Mr. Zakowski said stubbornly, "It is not good to trust too much."

"That's where I don't agree with you. I don't think there's enough."

The two men measured each other, the tall, kindly Martie Malone and the stocky, stern Polish father. . . . Oh, dear, Beany thought, this is where we lose Elena.

But Mr. Zakowski conceded, "Your way is not mine. I raise my children my way. But you are kind people. I give my consent for Elena to work for you. I hope you will not be sorry for not counting the money every night."

"I'm sure we won't," Martie Malone said.

Elena arrived at the Malones the next day at four-thirty. From that time on the home-coming Malones were welcomed by savory food smells. Lentil soup, beef roll-ups with a name only Elena could pronounce, fried pastries.

Martie Malone said to Beany, "That's another load off your mind—no worry over cooking or shopping. Now you'll have time to get to work on your pieces about Lilac Way. I've even got a typewriter you can take to

your room. One of the men at the *Call* left his with me
until he gets located. You won't have to wait your turn
at Johnny's or mine."

Beany moved the typewriter to a table in her room.
She pounded out, "Every good man must come to the
aid of his party," to get the feel of it.

But there was always some special event at Lilac Way
to occupy her mind. Beany got up from the typewriter.
After Thursday, she told herself, I can *really* concentrate.

Two Thursday mornings a month a teachers' club
used the Lilac Way pool. Carlton had told Beany, "Some
of them can swim. The ones who can't want to learn."

"Goodness!" Beany said.

Carlton gave her his slow smile. "Don't worry about
it. It's no different from teaching children—except leave
out the ducks and whales."

But Beany, accustomed for so many years to being
taught by teachers, felt uneasy about being the one to
say, "Do this—" or "No, that's wrong."

Carlton had added—but purely as Mr. Bull, director,
"You're doing a swell job, Beany. I heard about your
hauling out the little girl yesterday."

"Oh, it wasn't anything. She and her brother were
squabbling at the edge of the pool about which should
have one of those blown-up rubber ducks. She was

trying to tug it away from him, and slipped and kerplunked into the water."

No, Beany couldn't give herself much credit for that rescue. The little girl was but a few feet from the edge, and it took only a few strokes to bring her to safety. Yet Beany didn't relish overhearing Ofila say to a fellow Ho Ho, "So now Mees Bean is the great lifesaver. She brings in the very small child who has not more weight than a little puppy dog."

The cold war!

Beany's qualms about the teachers' club were quite unnecessary. They filtered out of the bathhouse, gay and friendly, and every bit as noisy as Beany's intermediates. Some could swim, and those who couldn't gave eager attention to everything Beany said.

This morning Beany came to unhappy grips with Ofila, who, as usual, was usurping the diving board. Not that the teachers wanted to dive, but the swimmers who paddled their way across the pool were made uneasy by Ofila's close dives and the waves that sloshed over them.

Beany approached the diving board. "Ofila, I'll have to ask you to stop diving while the teachers have the pool."

Ofila's satin-black eyes challenged Beany's blue ones. "Meestaire Buell has tell me I can dive whenever I want to dive."

"Mr. Buell also told you that the swimmers have the right of way, and you aren't giving it to them." She wanted to say a lot more— "Why don't you ever stay home and help your great-aunt with her traveling pain, instead of making life miserable for me?" Or even, "If you're trying to win Meestaire Buell's affection, you're barking up the wrong tree. I know—because I am, too."

There were even times when Beany, sensing the restless unhappiness of Ofila, felt a rush of sympathy. But not now—not with Ofila's mocking, "So I will tell Meestaire Buell that he is not the big boss here now since you tell peoples what to do."

Beany held back her angry, "Go ahead and tell him," and said only, "The teachers will have the pool until twelve."

Ofila stalked off, giving her a vengeful look. Beany went back to the beginning group and her routine about breath control and relaxation. But her own breath wasn't controlled, and she wasn't relaxed.

Was there a more *adult* way of handling Ofila?

20

BEANY thought of Andy Kern on the long bus ride home that evening. It surprised her that she had given but passing thought to him recently. She counted back in her mind; his leave had been up the previous Saturday. Strange, he hadn't called her.

She wished he would. She wished they could go dancing at Acacia Gardens. That's what she needed to break this foolish spell she was under about Carlton.

It seemed to her a most happy coincidence when she walked in the door at home, to have Mary Fred greet her, "Andy Kern just called. He's up at Father Hugh's at Twin Pines. He wants you to call him right away. He sounded kind of urgent. He told me not to let you go to sleep on the couch and forget. And I told him your days were back to normal because you passed the lifesaving test. Go ahead and call him."

Beany dialed the Twin Pines number. Andy's voice answered instantly. "Congratulations, Muscle Maid. Shall I genuflect or give you the Marine twenty-one-gun salute? Say, does a Malone car happen to be sitting in your driveway?"

"Yes, I noticed Adair's there. You mean you want me to drive up and get you?"

"That's part of it. But I've got something to show you and something to tell you, and I can't wait for you to get here."

Mary Fred, who was frankly listening, interrupted with, "You can take Adair's car. She said she wasn't going out."

Beany said into the phone, "Yes, I can come up in the convertible. Andy, this something you want to show me and tell me—will I be surprised?"

"I'm not sure. Sometimes I've almost told you, and maybe you—the sharpie that you are—have already guessed. Anyway, you burn up the road getting here."

Mary Fred was even more excited than Beany. "So he's got something to show you and something to tell you. Beaver, that sounds like a declaration of love and a diamond."

"For heaven's sake, Mary Fred. You've got diamonds on the brain since Dulcie—"

"But what else could it be? And up at Father Hugh's. I'll bet he went up there to talk it over with him first."

"Now look. Andy's still in the Marines."

"But not for long. I'll bet he's got a job all lined up, and is thinking of a cozy little nest for two. Gee, I hope he doesn't give you a diamond that isn't as big as Dulcie's."

Beany backed Adair's convertible out of the driveway onto Barberry Street, and headed west toward the mountains. Andy *had* sounded so urgent. Something to show her, something to tell her. What in the world? "Sometimes I've almost told you . . . ."

She reached back in memory to Andy's baffling soberness in the Malone driveway that rainy night. He had talked about crossroads. And his having a final date with Sylvia somebody so as not to leave any loose ends. He had wanted to find trees to chop down while he thought something over.

She stopped at a stop sign. Could Mary Fred be right?

There had been times when it had irritated Beany because Andy would have none of going steady. He had said, "I don't think that's the answer for kids in high school. Or for anyone, until they can start planning about who's going to sing 'Ave Maria' at their wedding."

249

Could Andy be waiting for her to talk over wedding plans with Father Hugh?

And what could Beany say? She'd hate to confess even to someone as understanding as Andy, "I'm far gone on Carlton. It's silly, because all I have to pin hopes on is one kiss. . . ." But it hadn't been a casual peck, Beany remembered—and her heart lifted at the memory.

She drove the thirteen miles on the highway to the foothills, and took the turn at Twin Pines that led to Father Hugh's stone church and rectory. She stopped the car on the sloping driveway. A man in clerical black was coming down the rectory steps and through the gate. She bent to pull on the emergency brake and thought fleetingly that Father Hugh must have a young seminarian visiting him.

She climbed out, lifting her eyes above the oncoming figure, expecting to see Andy come leaping down the steps and toward her. And then her eyes dropped and met the twinkling ones beneath the black biretta. She stumbled back a step, leaning against the car and breathed out an amazed, "Andy!" And that's all she could say.

"Don't just stand there with your mouth gaping open like a capital *O*. How do I look in a Roman collar?"

She couldn't answer.

He took her arm and gave her a little shake. "Why, Knucklehead, I didn't mean to bowl you over. I'm ashamed of being such a ham. But I thought you must have guessed what I was beating around the bush about a time or two."

"I never guessed." She was ashamed of how *wrong* she and Mary Fred had been.

He guided her toward the gate. "This is just a preview. I won't be wearing them for real until September when I enter the seminary."

And still Beany could only repeat after him, "Until September when you enter the seminary."

"The coat's new, and so is the biretta, but the rest of the outfit some priest outgrew and left with Father Hugh. He brought me up to try them on, and I wanted you to be the first to see me in them. Look. Black shoes, black socks."

Father Hugh was holding the door open for them. "Now, don't be blaming me, Beany, for proselyting. He was the one that came to me and said he wanted to be a priest. And I was the one who told him, 'It's nothing you can go rushing into. Wait, lad—wait, till you get to the point where the wanting to is bigger than you are.' "

A dazed Beany sat with them on Father Hugh's screened porch. She drank the lemonade his housekeeper brought, and tried to absorb all they were telling her.

251

Andy, Father Hugh said, was all for waiting the few months until his time in the Marines was up. Father Hugh, who knew his commanding officer, had only mentioned it to him.

"It was the C.O. himself who thought 'twas a pity that waiting would throw Andy here behind a year in starting at the seminary, and that as long as there was no war and the lad was only, you might say, marking time out there at Buckley Field—"

Andy put in, "And maybe the old boy was thinking about the times I gummed up telephone messages for him."

"Yes, maybe he was sick of the sight of you. But he took it up with the top brass, and they decided that in this case the U.S. service could give way to God's service. So he'll be having a new address in September. What do you think, Beany? Are you surprised, or did you feel it coming on? And are you happy about it?"

Tears filled her eyes and spilled down her cheeks. "Yes, I'm happy," she said on a choked laugh. "I don't know why I'm crying."

"That's the Irish in you. Ah, the tears my mother shed in pure happiness. The puckerin' string of her heart wasn't tight enough, she always said. And I say, look out for a woman that never sheds tears. . . . I wondered if you'd be surprised."

After the first jolt, Beany wondered why she hadn't guessed it before. This was what Andy meant when he had said, "Funny, how dreams can change. When I was a kid I wanted to be a police captain like my dad. . . . And then somewhere along the way, I got the idea—well, like Carl, that it was better to stop the hunger or the hate that made a fellow pick up a knife in the first place."

"Did you cut down trees and think it through?" she asked.

Andy nodded. "But I knew before I was halfway through the first tree."

Father Hugh was saying, "Look at him, sitting there grinning like a Chessy cat. He doesn't know the half of it. He'll have a harder life than most of us. He's the kind everyone will unload their troubles on every hour of the day and night. Let a boy land in jail or a man take to drink, and the first one they'll rout of bed will be the same Father Kern."

Beany laughed for the first time. Father Hugh was a great one to talk about the kind of priest everyone unloaded his troubles on.

Father-Kern-to-be stood up. "Now that I've knocked your eyes out, Beany, I'll get out of this hot, scratchy outfit."

Alone on the porch, Father Hugh hitched his chair out of the sun and closer to Beany's. "There's no heart involvement with you there, is there?"

"Oh, no. I've always thought so much of Andy—"

"And he's thought so much of you. You're luckier than most, child. Life is long and full of ups and downs, but you'll have one friend you can always turn to."

Beany's tears welled again. For suddenly she was given a glimpse of the years ahead and the kind of priest Father Kern would be. Not too different from Father Hugh. "A holy man and a fighting Irishman," Martie Malone described him. She could even glimpse an older Beany seeking comfort—"Andy, I'm so troubled . . . ."

He returned in his Marine summer khakis. Father Hugh picked up the lemonade glasses. "Now be off with the two of you. I've my breviary yet to say." He followed them to the gate, said as he always did, "Go with God," and with a quizzical lift of bushy eyebrows, "But not too fast on the curves."

At the car Beany said, "You drive, Andy. Can you stop off for dinner? You're sure of getting a good meal now that Elena is in the kitchen."

Not this evening, he said. It was his day off, but he'd promised to relieve a friend on the switchboard at Buckley Field.

Always afterward, Beany was to remember that drive back from Twin Pines in the twilight with Andy. Already the thought of his clerical garb separated them as boy and girl. Yet it drew them closer as human beings.

He told her of the need that kept growing in him until, as Father Hugh said, it was bigger than he was. "He wanted me to see what he called the *dreary* side of being a priest. That's why you didn't hear from me sooner. He had me down at his Mission helping with the down-and-outers. He'd thunder at me, 'You see, it isn't all adoring God.' As though I couldn't see that his cleaning up after some sick, old stumble-bum wasn't adoring God. Or even talking a storekeeper out of bandanas to take to your Ho Ho's."

"Oh, Andy, I keep thinking of your doing the Mexican Hat Dance the night our party was falling on its face!"

"Goose. You don't think I'll put on a long face when I put on the Roman collar, do you? If I'm in a black frock and things need perking up, I'll hitch it up and do the Mexican Hat Dance. And just think," he went on, "if you wait long enough to get married, I'll perform the ceremony gratis. But no, you'd have to wait seven—eight years. Well, I can baptize your kids."

"Don't count on it. I'm going to be an old maid. But full of good works. I'll take flowers to decorate the church for weddings—" Her laugh ended raggedly.

He stopped at a red light. His shrewd eyes searched her face. "Who is it, Beany?" he asked quietly. "Carlton Buell?"

A guilty flush drowned out her freckles. Not even to Andy could she confess her unrequited love. She hedged in what she hoped was airy unconcern, "I'd feel sorry for any girl that would fall for him. Because he—he isn't like other fellows. We've always laughed about it. How he freezes up if a girl starts pushing. How he always has to put a girl on a pedestal and—"

"Go on with you! What's the matter with his putting Beany Malone on a pedestal?"

"He knows me too well. He knows how I can lash out when I get mad—like that last night when he was driving me so hard before the test. I mean it, Andy, about being an old maid. I don't seem to have that whatever-it-is that men want to buy engagement rings for. Oh, sure, I'm good, old, helpful Beany. Trighorn feels so grateful, so big-brother to me. He brings me every new soft drink that Bartell puts out. He worries about my taking the bus and is always offering to drive me home. But it was Dulcie he went in hock for to buy a diamond."

"But would you want Trighorn?"

"Well, no. . . . Norbett Rhodes, too. Once we got over our mad infatuation, he took the good-old-Beany attitude. Just wait. As soon as it gets through his head that Dulcie's really giving him the air, he'll come running to me for sympathy."

Andy laughed heartily. "Not sympathy. Not Norbett. He'll come running, but he'll be very lordly about it all....But you don't want Norbett?"

"No, not Norbett."

He gave her a knowing look that all but said, "I know who you want," and patted her hand.

He stopped the convertible in front of his own house. His mother was working in her flower beds. Beany asked, as Andy climbed out, "What do all your folks think about your being a priest?"

"I've only told Mom and Dad. That's another thing, Beany, keep it under your hat for a while. It isn't official yet, not until my discharge papers come through. Dad's the closemouthed kind, and I threatened Mom to boil her in oil if she spilled a word to all the clan."

"Then I can't tell the family?"

"Not yet. I'll give you the word as soon as I get it." Again that knowing quirk of lips that was almost a smile. "You might mention to Mr. Bull at Lilac Way that Andy has a new love—which he has."

Beany had slid under the wheel. He reached through the car window and took her hand. "That heart you wear in your eyes, Beany—I want to see it happy. I want your life to be full of more than good works." He tilted her head and pressed a feathery kiss on her forehead. He added with his roguish grin, "After September it'll be only a fatherly—not a brotherly—pat on the back."

She started the car, and he waved her good-by from the first porch step. There he stood in his summer khakis, but already she was seeing him in his Roman collar and black coat.

As Beany drove into the Malone driveway, Mary Fred came running out the door to meet her. She hurried to pick up Beany's left hand. "What, no sparkler!" she exclaimed.

"No sparkler. No declaration of love."

"Fine thing. And here I told everybody I was sure you would come back with Andy and a ring."

"Well, you can just untell them. You didn't tell Elena, did you?"

"No, I didn't get around to telling Elena. Then what did Andy want to tell you and show you?"

"Oh—just something he and Father Hugh thought I'd be interested in," Beany evaded. "It has to be kind of hush-hush for a while."

Mary Fred said with a wise air, "I don't think I'll *un*tell anyone yet. You've got a sort of uplifted and mysterious look that I don't trust."

21

BEANY, going to her room after dinner the following Monday, heard the fast *clickety-click* of Johnny's typing. He was evidently trying to keep up with the words that were pouring out.

She sat down at the typewriter in her room, slid in a sheet of paper. After much thought she wrote a title,

A DAY AT A COMMUNITY CENTER

Not so good. Trite. She *x*'d it out and wrote,

THE MAKING OF A CITIZEN

and slowly pounded out a line, "There is a program to fit every need at the community center." Hm-mm. Not exactly what her father or Johnny would call eye-catching or elbow-jogging.

She put in a new sheet and tried a new heading,

IDEALS TO LIVE BY

and wrote, "Many young people—" She *x*'d out "people" and, thinking of the sticky-fingered Angelo, changed it to "boys." "Many young boys need guidance to learn that there is greater satisfaction in earning the things they want than by stealing them."

Good heavens! She was all but quoting Mr. Bull verbatim.

She got up from the typewriter and reached for a nail file and sawed viciously at her nails. *You've got to stop thinking about him,* she upbraided herself. *Haven't you noticed that already he's giving you the cool treatment? Maybe he's begun to notice that you're hunting excuses to go to his office. . . .*

She had this afternoon. She had said, "Carl, did you hear that the Hikers are reciprocating the Ho Ho's hospitality? They're having a barbecue for the girls next Saturday."

His slow smile built up to a chuckle. "Good enough. Beany, that fraternizing idea was one of the best you ever had. I'll bet the fellows will outdo themselves."

"I'll bet they'll outdo the girls. They're trying to guess what the fellows will serve. You are cordially invited, of course."

Beany waited. Now maybe he'd ask her if she was inviting Andy Kern as her date. And she would say, "Oh, no, Andy has a new love. I'll tell you all the details later."

Instead he said, "Yeah, it's better to have the fellows and girls mixing together here at Lilac Way instead of picking up dates on street corners. I'd like to see them carry on with their entertaining back and forth through the winter."

Again Beany waited to see if he'd say more about her working week ends at Lilac Way after school started. He had mentioned it several times when he was drilling her for the lifesaving test. But not a word.

In her upstairs room, Beany flung down the nail file. Yes *sir*, the sooner she got back into circulation and stopped mooning over Mr. Bull, the better.

Fate seemed to lend a hand in shoving her back into circulation. The very next evening at dinnertime when Beany answered the phone, a male voice asked, "Is this the home of the Miss Malone who took the lifesaving test at the Y?"

"Yes, I took it. I'm Beany Malone."

"Praise be. I've been going down all the Malones in the phone book. You're the seventh. That's seventy

cents' worth of devotion. I'm Jerry Burton—remember?
—one of your fellow bring-'em-in-or-busts that day."

"Of course I remember. Did you get your lifesaving
job in Boulder?"

"Yessum, I got it. And I got something for you. A
blue shoe. How come you did the Cinderella act on me
that evening?"

Beany murmured an explanation about being in a
hurry to get back to her community center.

"O.K. 'All is forgiven. Darling, come home.' How
would you like to go dancing tonight at Acacia
Gardens?"

She said fervently, "I'd love it, Jerry."

She meant, I'd love to dance and dance and not think
once about the boss out at Lilac Way. She dressed in her
best green brocade taffeta. And dabbed perfume on
generously.

Jerry Burton arrived in a low-slung sports car. He was
even better-looking than she remembered. A smoothie,
and a good dancer. After one length of the dance floor,
she caught his step and rhythm perfectly. When one
number stopped and they waited for the music to start
again, Beany did not edge away from the arm he kept
about her waist.

She was out for a cure, wasn't she?

At intermission they drank Cokes in the café that was part of the dance pavilion. Beany told him about her work at Lilac Way. "The melting pot, eh?" He grinned. "Don't you get yourself melted down in it, pretty babe."

He hitched his chair closer. "When I first looked at you, I was sure no girl could have as heavy eyelashes without their being glued on. I even watched to see what the water would do—"

"I use waterproof glue."

He reached for her hand. "I also checked to see if you wore some Joe's frat pin. I'm fond of freckles—yours look like Grapenuts."

She knew he said this—or the equivalent—to every girl he took out. But she teased him back. She didn't pull her hand away either. This was her night for forgetting.

And then, looking down the scattered tables, she saw Dulcie Lungaarde and Trighorn sitting in a corner. They were bent over the table and something Trighorn was drawing on a paper napkin—maybe showing her how he could block in her wall oven.

They were so happily engrossed, so oblivious of everyone else that Beany felt a pang of envy. That was the real thing, and this—this glib talk and hand-holding with a big wheel on campus was just phony imitation.

When Jerry said goodnight at the Malone front door, it took a bit of strong-arming on Beany's part to escape with just a casual kiss. Red's deep-throated grumble came to her assistance. Jerry took it good-naturedly enough. "The next time I'll say my fond adieus in the car."

Beany laughed, too, but she was thinking: There won't be any next time, Bud.

Lilac Way had a new volunteer worker four afternoons a week. He was a young chemistry teacher who was teaching rocket building to the boys.

"He's a godsend," Carlton told Beany. He meant that, with the interest in giraffes at a low ebb since virtually every home in a wide radius had one, this earnest, young man was taking up the slack perfectly with a new project.

On those four afternoons a week, Beany stepped around tables in the recreation room, covered not with laths and soggy newspapers but with balsa wood and strips of aluminum. The strong smell of banana oil sifted up the stairs to the clubrooms.

The godsend had shown an interest in Beany. Several times he had come early and gone into the pool where Beany taught. A short dip and then he stood, his shoulders swathed in a towel, to tell her of his other hobby—exploring old, ghost mining towns. Just a little enthusiasm on her part, Beany realized, and he would ask her to go on one of his Sunday junkets with him.

The next day after Beany's date with Jerry Burton, her excuse for going to Carlton's office was to show him one of Beverly's clay statues. She received the same courteous but very impersonal treatment.

Out of her hurt, her wanting to hurt him back, she did encourage the godsend. He did ask her if she were busy Sunday.

It came to her with a jolt that she would be paying dear for a very slim chance of hurting Carlton. She admired the godsend for his altruism in giving time to the boys at Lilac Way—but he did look pretty picked chicken in a swim suit. And the last thing she wanted was to go poking around some desolate, forsaken mining camp. She got enough of The Glorious Past from Johnny. So, as kindly as she could, she reached for the excuse of "something already planned."

Two evenings later, when sultry heat drove the Malones and Elena's iced coffee out under the chestnut tree, who should come swaggering around the house but Norbett Rhodes!

About a year ago, Norbett, playing the part of the up-and-coming young executive, had gone in for tweed jackets, expensive ties—even gloves. This evening he was coatless, in rumpled shirt and jeans, and his footwear could easily have passed for bath sandals. Under cover of the greetings and offering him a glass of coffee, Mary

Fred muttered to Beany, "I guess this is his beachcomber phase."

No, Norbett wouldn't sit down. He had found a record he wanted to take to a friend—and he was just passing by—and he wondered if Beany would like to go with him. Yes, Beany would. She hurried up the stairs, zipped herself into the apple-green linen sheath, and put on lipstick. And was rewarded by Norbett's grumble as he helped her into the car, "We're not going to a reception, you know."

Andy Kern's prediction was true. Norbett was very lofty about Dulcie Lungaarde and her engagement. He mentioned water seeking its own level. He hoped she and her plumber's apprentice would be happy.

"Plumber's apprentice, my eye! Trighorn practically runs Bartell's Bottling. He drives a swell car. You bet he and Dulcie will be happy. He'll be what is known as a good provider."

There, that ought to take Norbett down a peg or two! And yet the helpful side of her wanted to help him find his way. But how could she—or anyone—help when he didn't know where he was going?

He took her to the basement café where paintings, quite unintelligible to Beany, hung on the walls, and distorted bits of sculptoring sat about. They joined Norbett's friends who sat at a big corner table, drinking *caffè espresso*. These were the abused, the know-it-all, the angry young men, and the well-read but not well-dressed girls who had so disconcerted Dulcie.

Norbett had not only brought a record but a portable player for his poet friend in a dark turtle-neck sweater. They set up the player, and, to the jazz with a downbeat, the poet recited his own poem. It had to do with standing on the corner and seeing only "mangled roofs" and "cloven hoofs," and the practical Beany kept wondering how you could see both roofs and hoofs at the same time.

The *caffè espresso* kept Beany awake for an hour after she went to bed. Once, getting up for a drink, she glanced out the bathroom window. The light was still on in Carlton's room. She had a strong impulse to run through the hedge and call out to him, "Carl, they talk so much and don't *do* anything about anything."

That next day she and Carlton and Mrs. Harper ate lunch together on the grounds at Lilac Way. Beany asked, "Carl, have you ever read Dostoevsky?"

His eyes lighted. "Just about everything he wrote. He's one of my favorites. Someone said once, and it's true, that he had only one setting for every story—the human soul. And I like his two themes that he hammers away at. The all-guilt, meaning that all humanity shares the guilt of the thief, the murderer. And the other—you might call it a sort of *mysterium caritatas*. Meaning that kindness, compassion, forgiveness—just old everyday goodness is all-pervasive, too."

Beany reached for her bottle of Bartell's lime drink to wash down her sandwich. The bright boys she heard last night must have missed Dostoevsky's emphasis on such things as compassion and forgiveness.

"Funny, your mentioning him," Carlton went on. "Because I always think of how that *mysterium caritatas* of his applies to you—"

"To me?" Beany gulped on her swallow of drink.

"Yes. The way you make poor Eugene's day for him by wearing whatever crazy flower he brings you. The way you've softened the edges between the Ho Ho's and Hikers. You have sympathy and understanding with poor, mixed-up Ofila. That was what our Miss Joanne lacked. Just look at how Ofila has snapped out of her sulks and her tantrums."

Beany could only stare at him. Didn't Carlton realize that Ofila had snapped *back* into them? And that they were even worse on this second go-around?

"Did Ofila tell you I put her out of the pool the morning the teachers were swimming?"

"Yeah, and I told her I didn't blame you. She took it all right."

With you maybe, Beany thought. But not with me.

269

Mrs. Harper said, "I heard Ofila telling the girls that her uncle is out of hiding now and has opened his hotel again in Acapulco. Maybe he'll want her back for her Flame Dance and the dive from the rocks."

Carlton frowned thoughtfully. "I think 'Onkel' is running on a shoestring since his tangle with the government, and just plain hasn't the dough to send to her to come back. But I'm not so worried now about Ofila's adjusting. She seems kind of tense and restless but she's probably worrying about the Labor Day diving meet. She's pretty sure to win it. I keep looking around to see if I can find a job for her—you know, hostessing, or something comparable to what she did down there."

Mrs. Harper said nothing. And what could Beany say? Beany, who was in the same boat as Ofila. The boat that was getting exactly nowhere.

Beany had one more hope to break the spell she was under. Neither Jerry's amorous rush, nor the godsend's invitation, nor Norbett's willingness to include her in his carping circle had helped. Beany reasoned it all out. It was *Mr. Bull* she had fallen so hard for. And it was nothing but hero worship. That looking up to, that idolatry of everyone down at Lilac Way had rubbed off onto her.

Certainly she had never been heart-thumpy over good old Carl next door—Judge Buell's son and Johnny's best friend. That day she had gone into his house and eaten a sandwich in the sunroom with him had been no more romantic than if she had been with his mother.

If she could only move him back to being good old Carl and *not* Mr. Bull. Then her world would change back to its old serenity.

She hunted through the window seat and found some undeveloped film. She would ask him to print them for her—just as she had asked good old Carl so often in the past.

At dusk, when the station wagon in the driveway told her Carlton was home, she went through the opening in the high hedge and knocked on the side door. Anna opened it, and Beany said she would like to see Carl a minute if he was finished with dinner.

Mrs. Buell called out to her, "We're all through, Beany. Come on in and have a glass of iced tea with us."

Ah, this was even better than having Carlton come to the door. She would see him as the Buells' son. Maybe the judge, who didn't smoke, would be lecturing Carl for lighting a cigarette, and Carl would be looking sheepish.

The judge and Carlton both stood up when Beany entered the dining room. The metamorphosis might have taken place—Beany was never sure—if only Carlton hadn't stepped to her side and bent over to flick off some dead leaves that had stuck to her hair as she pushed through the gap in the hedge. His very nearness, his touch . . .

No, not even here was he good old Carl, not even when she said, "The next time you're making prints, I wondered if you'd do these three for me."

"Sure. I've got some in my camera I took of the Bombshells."

When she had drunk her iced tea, he walked across the lawns with her.

As long as he wouldn't turn back to good old Carl, she *made* conversation to hold Mr. Bull. About the Ho Ho's curiosity as to what the Hikers would serve. About the kitten that frisked about their feet. "I named her Eloise—I mean, she was the homely one nobody wanted, so I gave her a fancy name."

And when he turned away, Beany said—and hated herself for sounding wistful, "I miss riding to Lilac Way with you every morning."

He gave her an odd look. "I know. It's a long old ride on the bus. But I've still got my early-morning volunteers painting the gym. Good night, Beany."

"Good night, Carl. . . ." *Good night, Mr. Bull.*

Again that evening Beany set herself to writing the columns on community center activities which would counterbalance the ones on delinquency in the *Call*. Again she sat down to the typewriter Martie Malone was keeping for a friend. After fifteen minutes, she had written the first paragraph over three times.

She blamed her halting progress on the unfamiliarity of the machine, and her having to look each time for the dash or back spacer.

Johnny wasn't home. She went into his room to use his old model that wrote all the *e*'s as capitals and skipped a space or two whenever it felt like it. A story Johnny had written for the Pioneer Society contest lay on his desk. She picked it up and idly ran her eyes over the first lines.

She couldn't put it down until she came to "The End."

Finishing it, she had to look about her—at the desk lamp, the screened window—to get her present-day bearings. For she had been transported back to a "soddie" with homemade tallow candles and old blankets tacked over windows. Her hands even felt the soreness of the mother's hands from her constant wadding up of hay to thrust into the stove while a blizzard raged.

Martie Malone had said to Beany, "Take your reader right down to Lilac Way with you. Let him know those people."

Beany knew the people in Johnny's story. The wife with "her secret reservoir of hope." The man with his "leathery face crowfooted with wrinkles."

Beany had so much to tell, but, unlike Johnny, words didn't pour onto paper. They didn't even trickle.

22

THIS Saturday in August was to be an eventful day at Lilac Way. The Bombshells were to play their most important game that afternoon. The Hikers were putting on their cookout supper for the Ho Ho's in the evening.

Secrecy still surrounded the menu the boys would serve.

But so had the girls a surprise in store for their hosts. They had learned that today was the birthday of Waldo, the Negro guitar player, and there was much ado about making him a cake.

To make the whole event more gala, not only was Mr. Bull to be a supper guest, but he was to bring Miss Cirisi who would, in turn, present the second-place tennis trophy to Winnie. Sure enough, the cricket of Lilac Way

275

had been defeated by the girl from Carter Center with her "arms long as bed slats."

Anticipation of the evening ahead riffled through Lilac Way like a happy breeze.

In the late afternoon, when Beany guarded the pool and instructed the intermediates, she could hear the devout Maria practicing "Happy Birthday" on the piano. She glanced up now and then to the windows of the clubroom, sensing the busy excitement of the girls who were icing the cake. The ambitious Elena was even thinking of outlining a guitar in red icing on it.

Beany turned her attention back to her swimmers. She must tell Carlton that out of a class of twenty-two, all but four had learned to paddle the width of the pool.

Who am I, she thought wryly, to sneer at Ofila and her unhealed elbow when I'm always hunting for ways to get his attention?

Ofila, as usual, was at the diving end. This afternoon she hadn't dived and bobbed herself out of the pool and onto the board with her customary vehemence. She had dawdled between dives to talk to the hangers-on outside the mesh fence, or to imitate Beany again.

I won't let her get under my skin, Beany told herself, and went on coaching a round-faced boy who had a phobia about opening his eyes underwater.

Violetta was calling to her from outside the fence, "Miss Beany, come here. Because I have to tell you something."

"The class will soon be over," Beany called back.

But because Violetta insisted, Beany walked toward her. Violetta, with Vince hanging onto her skirt, was pressed against the mesh fence. "I want to tell you, Miss Beany—don't pay any attention to Ofila."

"I'm not paying any attention to her."

"Be sure you don't pay any attention," she repeated earnestly. "She is mean and I hear her talk—"

Two boys in the pool were having one of the constant disputes over an inflated inner tube. Beany settled it by taking it away from both of them and leaning it against the bathhouse. It was about time for the Bombshells to be returning from their game, and for Coach Magee to take over the pool for the players and the late swimmers.

But Beany had one more idea for inducing the round-faced Sammy to open his eyes underwater.

She went back into the pool and dropped into waist-high water a replica of the red plastic whistle she wore around her neck. "Look, Sammy, if you squat down and open your eyes for a minute underwater, you can see what I dropped on the bottom. And if you pick it up, you can have it."

He made three attempts, while Beany held back the others who were eager to duck down and grab the whistle. "Once more," Beany encouraged him. "Open your eyes with your fingers if they won't open themselves."

The fourth scrambling attempt, and he came up with the whistle and a look of such triumph that Beany jumped up and down and clapped her hands. So did all the others.

She climbed out and walked over to the corner by the bathhouse and picked up her towel. Such a small triumph, this getting Sammy over the first hump of being a swimmer. But she rubbed her head and wet shoulders with undue happiness.

She took off her dark goggles and surveyed the small world of Lilac Way. And suddenly it came to her in a revealing flash: It's so much easier for me to *do* things than to write about them. And I'm so much happier *doing*. Was that what Eve Baxter was trying to tell me?

Once when her father had been prodding her on those columns on community center activities, he had said, "If you don't write them, I will. I'll come down to your Lilac Way and get the lay of the land, and bang them out myself."

And he could. His observant eyes and heart would miss nothing. The right words would be there for him to reach for. If they weren't, they would come to him in the middle of the night. *But I'd rather think of other things besides words when I lie awake.*

She bent to rub her knees and thought, I'll tell Dad I'm no writer begging for a chance to prove it. I just thought I was. She waited to feel a pang of regret. There was none. She even chuckled softly as she said good-by to that woman novelist, Catherine Cecilia Malone, in her mink stole and orchid.

Dreams can certainly change, as Andy Kern said.

At the beginning of summer would she ever have thought that she'd be standing under an August sun by the side of a pool, brown and hard-muscled? And feeling quite at home on a tennis court, and in the kitchen and clubrooms of Lilac Way?

She thought ahead to the festive barbecue tonight—and the tempo of her heart changed. Andy's absence would certainly be conspicuous to Carlton, wouldn't it? He'd surely say, "Where's Andy, Beany?" and she would say, "Andy has a new love."

Would it make any difference to Carlton? Would he be all the more distant so as to keep the assistant at Lilac Way in her place? She leaned against the bathhouse and felt suddenly tired and heavy of heart. . . .

She was roused from her unhappy reverie by the chug, the final explosive snort of Coach Magee's jeep.

The first Bombshells were spilling into the park and making for the pool.

She blew the "all out" whistle to her class. She'd like to motion Ofila out, too. It wouldn't hurt the diving prima donna to give a hand to the Ho Ho's and the cake-making.

Ofila had just jumped from the five-foot tower onto the board and dived into the water. Unconsciously Beany glanced back, waiting for the black head to bob to the surface.

Her hand froze on her towel. A hand, clutching and unclutching, reached out of the water. The black head followed only long enough for a gurgled scream of "Help! Help!" and then went under again.

Even expert swimmers were sometimes stricken with cramp.

Beany took a running dive and swam to the spot. She had to dip underwater to see the black hair, and the figure in the red suit, doubled up on the bottom of the pool. Beany pushed herself down, grabbed the worn strap of the suit, and started to lift to the surface.

And then it was as though she had encountered a fighting tiger. Strong hands grabbed Beany by the shoulder, pulling her close, and at the same time, Ofila's knee was brought up with vicious force in the pit of Beany's stomach. Her double gasp drew a rush of water down her throat. She felt her hands and knees scrabbling on the bottom of the pool.

She fought her way up and floundered to the surface. She kept gulping for breath and each time she gulped water instead of air. She couldn't seem to do anything right. Her feet couldn't get the knack of treading water. Her strokes didn't tell. She'd lost all sense of direction. The bathhouse was at the wrong end of the enclosure. Somehow she threshed her way to the rail and grasped it.

Through her watery vision she saw that Ofila was already out of the water and standing close to the diving board. She was bending over the edge of the pool to taunt, "I think maybe I must save the life of our lifesaver."

Hand over hand, Beany made her way to the ladder and laboriously pulled herself out. She stood a dripping moment on legs that didn't feel like her own. Her head was puffed with water; every passageway in it ached.

Ofila, not at all the worse for it, taunted on, "I waited for the lifesaver to say, 'Ofila, save me!' And then I would keep you from drowning."

So that was it! Beany took a sick, confused look about her. She sensed the taut uneasiness of the ones pressed to the fence who had watched the ignominious performance. The usual stragglers. Even a few of the Ho Ho Club, who shuffled in either embarrassment or sympathy. Violetta was calling something, but Beany's ears were too blurred to catch it.

"That's what you wanted, wasn't it, Ofila? You planned it all just to make me look like a fool, didn't you?"

"You brag all the time about you are so wonderful lifesaver. It is laugh. I want to show Meestaire Buell you are no more good lifesaver than a goat. That is why."

Ofila stepped onto the diving board, and Beany followed her. The quiver of the board sent a wave of nausea over her. But anger—hot and searing—swept it aside.

She stepped close to Ofila and said between clenched teeth, "It was a skunky trick, Ofila. And it's the last one you'll pull. Because you'll never come in this pool again—not when I'm on the job lifeguarding it."

"How long you think you have this job? This job where you make the eyes of sheep at Meestaire Buell. I see you in his office holding him tight so he will kiss—"

It was purely reflex. Beany didn't know she lifted her hand until she felt the sting of it against Ofila's brown, wet cheek. Every ounce of her rage that had gathered during these months of Ofila's contempt and insults was in that slap.

Ofila reeled from the blow, and her wet feet slid on the board that vibrated jerkily under her. Beany backed

282

up a shaky step and held onto the rung of the low diving tower for support. It was only a second or two, but it seemed an interminable moment, that Beany watched the red-suited figure slithering—arms waving like windmills—as it tried to regain its balance on the wet bouncy board. Ofila fell in lopsided fashion on one knee, one hand groping wildly for a hold. She missed it—and Beany heard the thud of her head against the edge of the board as the distorted body tumbled into the water with a wide splash.

She watched with stupefied eyes for the water to settle, for Ofila to straighten herself out and bob up fiercely. She watched in growing horror to see the churned-up water carry the body out from the pool's edge—a body without direction or purpose.

Beany even looked around numbly—looked back. . . .

A second time Beany dived in after Ofila. And into a nightmare. The black hair and red suit was but a short distance from her, but each time she reached out she couldn't grasp it. It dipped underwater, rose again—while the water fought Beany back. She realized in dazed confusion that she was weighted down with the water she had swallowed.

At last she reached out and fastened her fingers in the thick, black hair. The hair hold. That would be easier and quicker. And that was all she had strength for. The

283

ringing of her ears was a din as she swam backwards, towing the body.

In shallow water, her feet groped for the bottom. She drew a ragged breath, and gripping Ofila's wrists and ankles, ducked under her and lifted her with the fireman's carry. Through shallow water, a doubled-over Beany plodded on leaden feet.

Ofila gave a small whimpering sound. She isn't dead, Beany thought dully. But the few feet to the end of the pool seemed a great, great distance.

Help came streaming through the bathhouse door and toward her. Coach Magee. Trighorn, who must have been delivering soft drinks for the party tonight. Mrs. Harper. Magee and Trighorn waded out and lifted Ofila off Beany's back. Mrs. Harper leaned over to help her up that one low step out of the pool. Like little Vince, Beany clutched weakly at a fold of the woman's skirt. She was dizzy and nauseated.

Magee and Trighorn carried their burden through the grounds, while Mrs. Harper guided the swaying Beany.

"Ofila's going to be all right," Coach Magee kept assuring them. "The kids said she hit her head a good whack. Probably knocked her out for a few minutes. But she's breathing all right."

Through a corner of the recreation room and into Carlton's office they went and eased Ofila onto the sofa.

"There, she's coming to," the coach went on. "Mrs. Harper, hand me the ammonia. Buell ought to be along any minute with Miss Cirisi. Take a good sniff of this, Ofila."

Ofila did. The eyes flickered open, turned slowly on each of the ones standing about her. They rested for a moment on Beany. . . . Her expression crumpled, and she sobbed out, "I want to go back to Mexico."

It was at this moment that Beany fled precipitately to the adjoining bathroom.

She vomited up the water she had gulped down when the knee had plunged with such force into her middle. The walls kept spinning around. Her stomach felt sore, and there was the rank taste of chlorine in her throat. Or was it the taste of shame?

That alley-cat scene at the pool! Ofila's loud taunts and Beany's slapping her. It was all so cheap, so degrading. Two girls fighting over Mr. Bull—while the same Mr. Bull went his busy way, quite unaware, quite uncaring about either of them.

Mrs. Harper pushed in to aid Beany, all troubled concern. She wrapped a towel around her shivering shoulders, kept soothing, "There now—there now. You'll feel better." And after a moment, "You wait here, and I'll get your clothes. You'll feel better when you get into something dry."

She came back with them and said, as she helped Beany dress, "Mr. Buell and Miss Cirisi are here."

"Here? You mean right here in Carl's office?" Beany said through chattering teeth.

"Yes, Miss Beany." She slid over Beany's tousled wet head the gay fiesta skirt Beany had brought to wear to the Hiker-Ho-Ho cookout tonight.

Hunted and desperate, Beany looked about her small quarters. If only the bathroom had an outside door so she could slip out. Without facing Carlton and Miss Cirisi.

She held onto the washbowl as though it were a life buoy, and chattered out in weak hysteria, "I want to stay here. Until Carl and Miss Cirisi leave the office. I've got to get away—if Trighorn is still here maybe he'll take me home. I—I don't want to tell them what happened—"

"They already know, Miss Beany. I told them."

"*You* told them?"

"Yes, I saw the whole thing. Your girls called me upstairs. They said Ofila had bragged that she was going to show you up, and they were worried about it. I was standing at the window looking down at the pool—and you know how clear the water is when the pool is empty. I saw Ofila pretending she needed to be rescued—I even saw her trying to knock you out in the water. I told Mr.

Buell. I never saw him so furious—why, he turned white. And I never heard such a lacing down as he gave Ofila."

"Did you—tell him and Miss Cirisi what happened afterwards—on the diving board?"

"I didn't see that. I heard Magee drive up, and I ran down to tell him to come to the pool with me." A smile flickered across her dark face. "Violetta filled in with the details of what happened afterwards."

Then Carlton and Miss Cirisi knew about the slapping. Dear Heaven, if only Violetta had left out what prompted it.

Mrs. Harper was buttoning Beany's blouse. "You come on now and lie down. I'll get a blanket to put over you. Mercy, you're all goose flesh."

Mrs. Harper opened the door into the office, all but propelled Beany through it, and pulled it shut behind them. She hurried softly through the office and out to her children in the recreation room beyond.

Beany leaned against the door, every freckle showing in her drained face.

287

23

BEANY'S blurred vision saw that Miss Cirisi, in a dressy print, was standing by the desk. Carlton sat on a corner of it, talking on the phone. He dropped it and hurried to Beany, his eyes searching over her. "You all right now? You sure? Here, sit down—no, lie down on the couch."

Miss Cirisi came to take her other arm.

The leather couch was empty. Beany sat on it, and her eyes focused next on the girl she had last seen lying on it.

Ofila was on her feet. She leaned against the water cooler, holding a compress to the swelling bruise between temple and ear. She was still in her shabby, red swim suit, but a towel was around her shoulders, and someone had brought her one of her tiered skirts to put on. Its ruffles hung limp about her bare ankles. She looked chastened and, like Beany, as though she wished she were anyplace else but here.

Carlton tucked his own sweater around Beany, repeated, "You sure you're all right? I'm just talking to Emily. She and Uncle Matt are planning on driving to Mexico to get the folks there. I want to see if they can take Ofila with them."

It took a minute for Beany's dazed mind to absorb that. Then Uncle Matthew *had* decided to drive down to Mexico City and get his wife and other daughter.

Miss Cirisi was saying, "You'll be a lot happier down there with your own people, won't you, Ofila?"

Ofila didn't answer her but looked at Carlton and asked, "Is it *you* want me to go back to Acapulco?"

He reached out and took the compress from her, dampened it with water from the cooler. "Hold that on a little longer—it'll keep down the swelling—and then I'll put ointment on it. . . . Yes, Ofila, because you can't seem to make a life for yourself up here. I guess you realize that by now."

Beany lowered her eyes. That was Carlton's answer to Ofila's foolish hopes. Ofila knew now that she had been only another Violetta, another Eugene that Meestaire Buell had been kind and helpful to. . . . *I know exactly how you feel,* Beany thought on an ache of sympathy.

289

Carlton added, "You told me that your uncle and cousins wanted you to come back."

"Ah. They will be much glad to see me. They will throw arms around me and say, 'Ofila, Ofila, we have miss you. Now you are come to do the Flame Dance and the long dive from the rock.' "

Pride, Beany thought admiringly—Ofila's got that. I'm going to need all I can scrape up, too.

Carlton picked up the phone and carried on his conversation with his cousin Emily. He replaced the phone and relayed the conversation they had heard scraps of. "Emily will be taking her little boy. She'll have to talk to her father about your going with them, Ofila, but she said she'd like to have you along. Neither she nor Uncle Matt speak Spanish, and I told her you'd be a help in ordering meals and getting hotel accommodations on the way down. Emily said that if Uncle Matthew could wind things up today, they might even leave tomorrow. Could you be ready by then?"

Ofila nodded. "I will have the suitcase packed. My great-aunt will be glad for me to go. She was not made happy by me in her so little house. She goes to bed early, and I was never go to bed early when I am with my uncle and big family in the hotel." As she talked, a happy anticipation seemed to build up in her. "In Acapulco, night times is time for everybody to be happy."

"Now remember, Ofila," Carlton went on, "you're to make yourself agreeable to Uncle Matt and Emily. None of your acting high and mighty. You *sabe*?"

"I *sabe*. I will be glad inside to go and I have more glad all the time I get closer to home. Only when I am not glad inside I am—what you say—high and mighty. Maybe you will help me to send post card by airplane to tell them I am coming. They will all be waiting—" Her anticipation by now had put a glow in her dark eyes. "They will be surprise at how good I speak the English, and how I win two trophies up here in Colorado. I can take what I win that is upstairs on sideboard, yes?"

"Sure, your trophies and pictures and write-ups," Carlton told her. "Here now, I'll cover that bruise with ointment."

Ofila's pride, Beany knew, prompted her next remark. "In Acapulco where I dive the best, in Mexico City where I sit in the president's box at bullfights, many men will ask me to marry."

Carlton chuckled. "I'll bet they will. One a day at least. You keep this ointment, Ofila. By the time you hit Mexico, you'll be as good as new."

Mrs. Harper came to the door to tell Carlton that Coach Magee was waiting to see him.

Carlton turned in the doorway to say, "Don't leave till I come back, Ofila. I want to take you home and explain to your aunt about your going back to Mexico with Uncle Matthew."

Ofila was the first to speak when Carlton was gone. "Now I will go upstairs and get the silver trophies and the pictures off the walls. Because in my uncle's hotel I will put them up for all peoples to see."

As she turned to leave, Miss Cirisi said shortly, "Wait a minute, Ofila. Don't you think you ought to apologize to Miss Beany for acting like a vixen and trying to drown her? And thank her for saving your life when you knocked yourself out falling into the pool?"

"That was my fault," Beany said quickly.

"The fault was mine," Ofila put in. "I give apology from my heart. Now I am happy, I have grief for making you unhappy, Miss Beany."

"I give you apology, too, Ofila—from my heart. I hope you'll be happy down there with all your folks."

Beany reached out her hand, and Ofila took it. She said, with her eyes on Beany's wan, troubled face, "I would wish happiness for you also. It was not that I did not like you, Miss Beany, it was only—only that you made mad in me when—" She shrugged meaningfully, added, *"Adios,"* and, totally ignoring Miss Cirisi, ducked out of the room.

Miss Cirisi broke the awkward moment of silence when she and Beany were left alone in the office. "It's so easy for us Americans to think that anyone can adjust to our ways. But every now and then we find someone who can't."

"I guess so," Beany murmured, and waited for Miss Cirisi to get to the slapping incident.

"I never did think Ofila would. It was too much of a change. There's something on her side, too. Her old aunt was ailing and wasn't at all pleased at having Ofila dumped on her hands. Carlton kept hoping that we could find a job that suited her. But where in dry-land Colorado is there a spot for a dancing-diving star? I guess he finally realized it himself."

Was all this talk about Ofila just stalling for time? Beany had to get it over. She said, "I was to blame for slapping her today. I guess you've—I mean, I won't blame you for firing me. I—don't know what made me—do such a thing."

A laugh could be sober and rueful. Miss Cirisi's was.

"It isn't the sort of treatment I'd recommend to our workers. But there's such a thing as being driven to it, Beany. Mrs. Harper told us what happened in the pool. She's told me before about Ofila's needling you. Even Miss Kunitani was worried about it before she left. . . No, I'm not going to fire you. You've done too good a job here at Lilac Way. I don't see why you and Carlton can't carry on a program together here this winter when you're both in school."

Beany managed a grateful, "Thank you, Miss Cirisi." But she was thinking: You don't know Carlton Buell the way I do. You don't know how lordly he was with Miss Joanne because she wasn't adult enough to handle Ofila. And *she* didn't even come close to slapping her. No, I certainly slapped myself right out of Lilac Way—and Carlton's life.

Sometime, Beany thought on, when my head isn't ringing and I can talk without crying, I'll ask Miss Cirisi to transfer me to one of the other centers. Or maybe Carlton will beat me to it and ask for another assistant here.

A soft knock at the door, and Mrs. Harper came in with a cup of steaming tea. Behind her was a knot of the Ho Ho's wanting to inquire about Miss Beany. Beany caught Elena's anxious, blue eyes and said, "I'm just fine."

The Ho Ho's also shyly invited Miss Cirisi to come up to the clubroom and see their surprise birthday cake. Miss Cirisi stood up. She patted Beany's arm. "You drink your tea and then catch a little nap so you'll be in shape for the festivities later on."

Beany sat alone in the office in which no one had thought to turn on a light. Even the scalding sips of tea could not wash the taste of chlorine and shame out of her throat.

Mrs. Harper came in again to pick up the empty cup. "Lie down and rest now, and I won't let anyone else come bothering you. Mercy, child, you're still shivering." She tucked the blanket around Beany and went out, closing the door softly behind her.

Lying there, Beany could hear the bang of doors in Carlton's station wagon, the whirr of the starter. Mentally she followed the car to the little house on the back of the lot where Carlton in his fluent Spanish would explain to the old lady about Ofila's sudden leave-taking for Mexico.

He was certainly losing no time in disposing of Ofila. She was the lucky one. She'd had her lacing down. She was getting away from it all. It would be easier to forget Mr. Bull in Acapulco.

Beany lay in the dim room and heard the activity going on in the old brick house. Hurried footsteps in the clubroom overhead. The familiar titter as the gigglers passed the office door. . . . Father Hugh had said, "Ah, laugh while you can. The day will come when you'll think you'll never laugh again. . . ." That day had come for Beany.

By now the Hikers would be starting their fire in the outdoor fireplace for cooking their mysterious *pièce de résistance.* And Miss Beany, leader of the Ho Ho's and instigator of these cookout parties, lay in sick dread of Mr. Bull's return.

She fell into a heavy, troubled sleep. In it she was fighting against water. She was swimming without making progress—and straining, straining to reach something which was beyond her grasp. Her heart was thudding in panic . . .

Suddenly the dream changed. In the new dream, the outside door of Carlton's office opened, and someone came hurrying across the scabby linoleum and dropped down on the lumpy sofa beside her. Both her hands were clasped in warm, strong ones while a voice said, "Beany, is it true? She told me you slapped her because you loved me—and that I was dumb like a donkey not to know—"

In the dream Beany's voice answered, "It's true."

"But I thought it was Andy. I started loving you that day I found you sitting on the park bench looking so kicked-in-the-teeth."

In that drowsy state between sleep and waking, she murmured, "It's not Andy. It's you. And I don't know when I started loving you—but Johnny always said you'd go into deep freeze if—"

It was his swift swooping her into his arms that brought her to wide awakeness. Again she heard his excited, exultant laugh—and again she returned the kisses and felt his heart beating under his hard ribs. Even the same smell of liniment.

Again they were both talking in a foolish hysteria where words wouldn't come fast enough. "I didn't mean to slap her. And the minute I did, I could just hear you telling me it wasn't very adult—"

"But darn human. I all but clouted her on the other side of her face when I heard what she'd done. And when I heard from Violetta about her 'making faces,' and from Mrs. Harper and the girls how she's been pouring it on you— Oh, Beany, I have been dumb like a donkey not to know what went on around here."

"No—just naïve as the Bobbsey twins." And Beany, who had been sure only a short time ago that she would never laugh again, laughed and cried at the same time.

And then silence. Later on would be time enough to talk over week-end programs for Lilac Way and to ask Carlton what courses she should take at the university. Oh, yes, later on they would talk about how surprised their families would be. She would even tell him about Dulcie's advice to latch on to him before someone else did.

But now it was enough to sit within the haven of his arms, to answer his, "Beany, beloved, your hands are like ice," with a low, "They're warm in yours. . . ." She thought of Andy calling her knucklehead or doll or sugar. There had been an extravagant Italian boy that even called her St. Cecilia and the sun in his fog. Carlton wasn't the kind to toss about endearments. He would call her "beloved" or "sweetheart," and his very seriousness would add a special depth and meaning to their love.

He was saying, "I'd like to shout it from the housetops," and she answered on a soft laugh, "You'd better wait and shout it to our families first."

Yes, all that would come later. Now it was enough to feel the world shut out. . . .

But again the world pushed in. A small rectangle of light, as the door from the recreation room was opened, became a larger rectangle that caught the two sitting on the couch. Carlton stood up, blinking in the sudden brightness.

It was Violetta and, of course, her shadow and echo, Vince.

"The fire is burning," announced the reporter at large, "and Eugene has gone again to the cemetery and is holding for you, Miss Beany, a flower he got off Luigi's grave—remember Luigi that was shot by a cop?"

"Cop," came the echo.

"And the Miss Cirisi lady said please to bring out the trophy that is wrapped on your desk. Right away, because she is ready to give it to Winnie that would have won first, except for the girl from Carter Center with her arms long as— "

"O.K., O.K.," Carlton said. "You run along and we'll be right out."

"I have more to tell you," she said reproachfully. "I know what the surprise is the boys are cooking. It is barbecued ribs that they put ketchup on. I thought you would want to know."

Beany and Carlton glanced at each other. As though it mattered to them whether barbecued ribs or stewed seaweed were served to them tonight.

"And everybody is asking if Miss Beany is all better enough to come to the party, because Eugene says it will not rain and the moon will shine."

Beany threw aside the blanket and got to her feet. "Yes, Violetta, tell them I'm all better now. You'd better take the trophy out, Carl. Give me just five minutes to comb my hair."

"I'll be right back for you," he said.

But it wasn't only for combing her hair that she wanted those few minutes alone in the darkening office. She wanted to absorb, to savor the wondrous knowledge, *Carlton loves me*. She wanted the happiness of listening for his footsteps and thinking of the years ahead when she would be listening for them. . . .

She was even greedy enough to want that extra dividend of joy as he came in and said, "Ready, Miss Beany?" and gathered her to him, and ruffled the hair she had just combed.

About the Author

Lenora Mattingly Weber was born in Dawn, Missouri. When she was twelve, her adventurous family set out to homestead on the plains of Colorado. Here, she raised motherless lambs on baby bottles, gentled broncos, and chopped railroad ties into firewood. At the age of sixteen she rode in rodeos and Wild West shows. Her well-loved stories for girls reflect her experiences with her own family. As the mother of six children and as a grandmother, she was well qualified to write of family life. Her love of the outdoors, her interest in community affairs, and her deep understanding of family relationships helped to make her characters as credible as they are memorable.

Mrs. Weber enjoyed horseback riding and swimming. She loved to cook, but her first love was writing.